THREE MEN HAD BEEN KILLED.

And maybe I'd be number four. I guess the job was worth it.

The man we had to get out of China had a packet of top Chinese secrets in his top British brain.

That's why I was in this hideout hotel behind the Bamboo Curtain, meeting the man's mistress in the bar. "How do you do?" she said. "I am Chang Choy-lin."

Upstairs she swung the door open and I slid to one side with my back against the wall. At first I didn't see him. Then I saw him—huddled in a corner, peering at me through a shock of graying hair. "I want my nanny," he said. "I want my nanny."

Chang Choy-lin looked at me. "He's insane," she said.

The Dragon's Eye

Scott C. S. Stone

A FAWCETT GOLD MEDAL BOOK
Fawcett Publications, Inc., Greenwich, Conn.

For
BARBARA
with love

———————— one

WE WENT TO ASIA.

We stepped down from an airplane one fire-colored morning and looked out over a harbor filled with sails, and we breathed the incense and noise while Asia broke over us in long, deep rollers, like the tide on a sandy beach. That was nearly twenty years ago and we were new to it, and young.

In those days in Asia we knew colors of green and umber and scarlet, knew gongs and cymbals, knew an Asia that tinkled like a temple bell. Before very long the colors became the peculiar gray of blown buildings and the scarlet of blood. The sounds became mortars and the count of the executioner, and a whisper of warning in the hot, humid night.

Not in the beginning. In the beginning we were schoolboys on a holiday, exuberant and restless. Asia was a lark; it was ours. Its girls and history and magic evenings were ours. That was once upon a time, and it never came again.

We became war-wise and war-weary. We went into combat and came out the other side with memories of fatigue and frostbite and the kind of fear that dries your mouth and makes your genitals ache. We watched the countries changing, old civilizations being reborn in the manner of things in Asia. We watched history take shape and we dutifully reported it, writing long pieces on the metamorphosis of the East.

War and time and experience: they all led us, finally, to Saigon and still another war, and we had been in it nearly two years when one of us was killed.

I had become more cynical than Jerry Ward. I handled my share of operations, but I didn't go out with green troops.

He did and it got him killed. I didn't hear about it until I showed up at the daily five-o'clock briefing. I raised hell with the public information officer for not telling me first—Jerry was in my bureau, after all—and rode back to the office on Nguyen Hue with a dull feeling between my eyes. I cabled the story and went out again and up to the fifth floor of the Majestic at the end of Tu Do Street, and sat there drinking. Near Cu Chi, not far from Saigon, some kid stepped on a mine and four people died, Jerry among them. He never would have stepped on a mine. He was very canny, very careful, except for that willingness to go into combat with untested troops. They said he died instantly. They always say that, but it's damned rare.

I drank my way steadily around town. It took me a long time to get drunk and I began to think I wasn't going to make it, but I did. It happened in a dirty bar in Cholon, full of noise and smoke. I sat there and drank and watched the overhead fan turn so slowly the flies were riding on it, unafraid. I put my head on the bar and listened while the sounds creept in and vibrated near my ear, telling me of the long years in Asia, and friends gone, and love gone because there was a story to be filed somewhere, a deadline to be made.

I made an epic journey away from the bar and reached my flat. I called the office.

"I'm drunk," I said. "I'm not coming in."

The next day I went in and called a meeting. I turned the bureau over to the night editor and cleaned out my desk. I cabled my resignation to New York and said good-bye to the staff, then went home to pack. After nearly twenty years I didn't own anything I couldn't carry in one bag. If I had thought about it long enough, it might have bothered me, but all I wanted then was just to get the hell out of Asia.

I got as far as Hawaii.

Clear-eyed and sober, I had boarded a plane at Tan Son Nhut. Just before we took off, I saw helicopters coming back from a mission, one of them coming straight in, hurriedly, probably with wounded on board. Good-bye to that, I said, and immediately added that cynical catchall phrase so popular in Vietnam: sorry about that. We took off and I fell asleep and when I was awake again, we were landing in Manila, a place I disliked. I watched the tourists buying wood carvings made back in the barrios and jewelry made in Bangkok. I watched the heat waves rising from the concrete runways and then crawled gratefully aboard a jet and after we were airborne, I watched appreciatively while a long-legged American stewardess poured champagne.

For only the second time in nearly twenty years I was going back to America and I began to build it up in my mind, not the prosperity and all that but the little things. I wanted to buy cigarettes out of a machine instead of sending a houseboy out for them, and watch television, and walk across a park without thinking about where the machine guns would be placed for maximum effectiveness. And I wanted to work on a book about Asia, knowing in advance it was impossible to get it all in and, knowing it, still wanting to try. There were some things I wouldn't put in, though.

Guam to Wake to Honolulu for a most welcome layover. I liked Honolulu from an earlier, short visit, and while they were building hell out of it, they couldn't take away the sea and the mountains and the magnificent sunsets.

I got a cab into town, went down and holed up at the Halekulani on the beach. Two days later I was still there, charmed by the Islands—at least by what I could see from a rented car—and after I'd been there a week, I started reading the classified sections, searching for a house.

Six months after Jerry was killed I was living in a cool and airy house in Manoa, working happily and diligently on a book. I had a lanai on two sides of the house and I could sit out there and drink and look down the valley toward the sea or slightly over my shoulder toward the mountains. In the back was a mango tree and the front lawn was full of plumeria, and in one eave of the house I had a nest of lovely little green birds with white circles around their eyes. I was tanned and healthy and not drinking too much and learning to surf. There was unbeatable sunshine and a weekend now and then on another island for a change of pace.

And there was Joan.

She had an ex-husband she still loved and was trying to forget. Unsuccessfully. There was someone in Hong Kong I was trying to forget as well, but what we had known kept coming back to me without warning, and I would never forget her.

Joan and I made love the night we met. It was almost an

accident; we saw the need in each other's eyes and just got on with it, without pretense and without preliminaries. After that she came to my place more or less regularly, but we never pretended it would last, or even that it should. It took care of her sexual needs and mine, and now and then we went away together to another island. It was an affair without any strings on either of us and the best that could be said for it was that we didn't take it seriously. But it was fun.

Then there were footsteps on the lanai shortly after dusk one evening and moments later the doorbell rang. For all that followed that soft doorbell should have been a cannon shooting through the door, but I didn't know it at the time.

I opened the door and looked up at Leslie Trent.

"Hallo, Hawkins, you old bastard," he said, grinning.

"You damned limey. Come in."

It was good to see him again. We had knocked around a lot of places, Jerry and Leslie and I, and we had a great deal of affection and respect for each other. Leslie was a very fine newsman, with a keen sense of history, a knack of telling readers not only what was happening but what it all meant.

I went out to fix drinks, without having to ask what kind. In all the years I'd known him he never drank anything but gin-tonic and if he couldn't get it, he'd go without.

I brought the drinks back and sat in a chair opposite him. He hadn't changed much. He was a couple of inches taller than I and slender and very handsome. He was English and looked a little like Peter Lawford. He had trouble keeping women away from him, but he never really tried very hard unless he was working, and then he was all business, a driving competitor who would joke with you one minute and beat you on a major story the next. He took his job seriously. I liked him very much.

"A nice place," he said.

"Expensive," I said, "but very private."

"Cheers."

"Cheers."

"You planning to stay awhile, I suppose?"

"Absolutely. I'm hacking away at a book and I'm to the point where I can stand up on a surfboard. I can't leave at a time like this."

"I was in Java when you left Saigon. Surprised me a bit. Was never sure why you left."

"I got tired, that's all, and Jerry got killed and I said the hell with it."

"I see."

"Well, the hell with it. What about you? What are you doing here?"

"Just visiting," he said, and gave me a slow smile.

"Oh, Christ. If I were still working, I'd start to worry."

"Well don't worry, chum. I'm out of the news game myself."

"You left Reuters?"

"Yes. Not long ago."

"What are you doing now?"

"I'm a retired journalist. Meaning I'm an out-of-work newsman. I'm just coasting around a bit. But tell me about Jerry. I read the UPI version of it. Know any more?"

I told him what little more I knew and we were silent for a few minutes, thinking of Jerry, and I got up to fix a second round. When I got back, Leslie was standing and looking out my window.

"Nice view, Michael," he said.

I stood beside him at the window. I pointed out the university, and the Ala Moana building down near Waikiki. But as I talked I began to sense he wasn't interested.

"Tired, Leslie? Of course you're staying with me. Where's your gear?"

"I've got my kit out in the car," he said. "Rented car. I knew you'd invite me to stay over unless you had some hula girl panting in the bedroom." He paused. "There isn't anyone, is there? Really close to you, I mean. You aren't in love or anything like that, I hope."

I looked straight into his deep blue eyes. "Why do you ask? What's going on?"

"Let's sit down," he said. "This is going to be a little complicated."

"I don't think I'm going to like it."

He smiled again. He had a nice smile, reaching his eyes. "Well, Michael, it's obvious your instincts are as good as ever."

He sat on the couch and put his drink on the coffee table and leaned forward with his elbows on his knees. I sat back in a chair straight across from him and waited. There was a familiar little buzzer going in the back of my head and it kept signalling *watch out, watch out.*

"Michael," he said. "I want you to remember something. I want you to go back, to 1951. Where were you then?"

"Korea," I answered. A lifetime ago.

"All right," he said. "I had just met you then, remember? But we didn't know each other very well. I was knocking about with the Canadians and the Black Watch and you were with the Marines."

"Yeah," I said, remembering. "The Fifth Marines, up on the Imjin River mostly."

"Then you were at Panmunjom."

"Right."

"Covering the truce talks."

"Right."

"And doing something else."

There was a pause. "All right," I said. "Tell me."

"You did a job for Army Intelligence."

I didn't say anything.

"I'll read it to you," he said. He reached in his jacket pocket and pulled out a folded sheaf of papers.

"Listen to this," he said, and started reading:

"Nam Il, general, North Korean People's Army . . . senior delegate . . . returned to Korea in 1932 as a university graduate and engaged in a clandestine underground movement until 1942 . . . teacher in Russia until the end of 1942 . . . in 1948, elected to the Supreme People's Assembly . . . chief of the general headquarters, Social Security Ministry Detachment, corresponding roughly to the U.S. Central Intelligence Agency . . .

"Kim Il Sung, premier of North Korea and commander-in-chief . . . original name was Kim Song Ju, born in Taedon Gun, Pyongan Namdo, in 1911 . . . Soviet Colonel Ignatoff, Deputy of Romanoko, North Korea Civil Affairs Headquarters, addressed a meeting and stated that it was his pleasure to introduce to the gathered Communist leaders the national hero and outstanding guerrilla fighter, Kim Il Sung. Kim then stepped to the platform dressed in civilian clothes, wearing a row of Soviet decorations, and introduced himself as Kim Il Sung, member of the Chinese Communist Party . . . represented North Korean Labor Party when the U.S.—U.S.S.R. Joint Commission met in Pyongyang . . .

"Peng Teh Huai, commander of Chinese Communist——"

"All right, Leslie," I interrupted. "Now tell me what it means."

"You wrote those reports. Agents brought the information to you and you put it together. You were a natural for it; you could write well and you were on the scene at Panmunjom and the U.N. delegates liked and trusted you. One night you were called to the tent of the senior U.N. delegate. He asked if you'd take some time off and put together biographies of the delegates from the other side, then forget you'd ever gotten involved. You agreed and the information poured in. You moved from the press train down at the railhead into a tent at Munsan-ni, near the headquarters tent. It took you exactly eight days to put it all together. The U.N. delegates were pleased with it. They were happy to get a little insight into the men opposing them. You didn't mind doing it and when it was finished, you forgot about it."

"Until now." The warning buzzer was about a hundred decibels higher.

"Until now," he echoed.

"Let's have another drink," I said. "I have a feeling I'm going to need it."

I went out in the kitchen and fixed two more, my mind working all the time. His information was precise. And I had forgotten about it. It was a minor thing and a long time ago and I hadn't gotten involved in any damned intelligence stuff since. I knew a couple of agents here and there—they aren't hard to spot in the Orient, particularly if you're a newsman with a built-in mistrust—but I stayed away from them and they stayed away from me. And now Leslie, right up to his ears in some kind of operation. Well, he wasn't going to involve me, and the old warning signal told me that was exactly what he wanted. I walked back into the living room and handed him the gin-tonic. He was still sitting on the couch and he looked up and gave me a sort of rakish grin.

"Are you scared now?" he asked.

"Damned right. But curious, too, and a little disappointed in you."

"Why?"

"You come swinging in here, obviously a damned spy, lugging around information you could have gotten only from some military intelligence apparat or the C.I.A. and you're setting me up for something because of a minor job I did as a favor a long time ago. I don't like it and the answer is no, before we get in any deeper and you tell me stuff I shouldn't hear and don't want to hear."

"You're jumping to conclusions."

"Am I? Am I really?"

"No."

"Then, let's knock it off and talk about something pleasant. Women, maybe, or surfing. You want to learn to surf while you're . . . visiting?"

He looked at me in annoyance. "Don't make it difficult for me, Michael."

I felt very tired all of a sudden. I put my head in my hands and whispered, "Why me?"

"Because you've been asked for," he said. "By name."

"By somebody in Washington, I suppose, or London?"

"No," he said. "Somebody in Peking."

"Sorry Leslie," I said. "I just don't think I know anyone in Peking."

He walked up and put a hand on my shoulder. "I'm sorry to be the one to do this to you. I told them you wouldn't like it, that I didn't want to do this to you. Then I got ordered to do it, and now I'm doing it, but I don't want you to think I like it."

I believed him, but that didn't help much.

Finally I could hear my voice, flat and unemotional, asking what they—and who were they?—wanted me to do.

"I can't go any further until you've agreed to work with us," he replied.

"You're asking me to do something I won't like, but you won't tell me what it is until I've agreed to do it." I almost snarled at him.

"That's right," he said.

"Why does it have to be me, for God's sake?"

"I told you. Because you were asked for. Because you're the only one that can do it."

"Why?"

"I can't tell you until you agree to do it," he said patiently.

"And what makes you think I'll agree?" I could hear the rasp in my voice. I liked Leslie. Next to Jerry he had been my closest friend for years, and it wasn't really anger I felt but bitterness.

"You have to do it, Michael," he said. "You have to do it because you're the only one that can do it, and because it's necessary that somebody do it, that it be done."

"Leslie, is there any way——"

"There isn't," he interrupted. "There's no other way."

I sat down and swore under my breath. Then I surren-
dered: "All Goddamned right," I said. "What do I have to
do?"

He got right to the point: "At Panmunjom you met an
Englishman, only he was covering the war from the other
said. Remember Malcolm Leigh? Wrote for the *London
Daily Worker*, *L'Humanité*, a few others?"

"Sure," I said. "Haven't thought of him in years."

"He stayed on in Korea for a bit, then went to China. He's
in Peking now, a very high-placed official with the Hsinhua—
you know it as the New China News Agency—and a rather
powerful figure in the Politburo of the Chinese Communist
party. He wants to come over."

"Come over?"

"Defect. Leave China. By way of some Asian port."

"I don't understand what that's got to do with me."

"He won't defect to anybody but you."

"Are you kidding?"

"No," said Leslie. "We want you to go out and bring him
back."

two

I WAS TOO SMART TO GO UP ON OAHU'S
north shore. The waves up there hit twenty feet on a good
day, and they had a lot of good days. People got wiped out
and there was a lot of rock and coral. When you got a coral
cut, it lasted for weeks. The rocks were all lava, and if you
hit one of them, you knew you were hurt. Sandy Beach, out
past Makapuu, was a lot better and I went there sometimes.
I was getting better all the time, but I was no Duke Kahana-
moku, so on the morning after Leslie showed up at my place,
I tied the board on top of my car and drove down to the
beach at Ala Moana. It was a lot more tame there and not as
crowded as Waikiki or Diamond Head.

I paddled out past the reef, feeling the strain on my

shoulders and along both sides. The surf wasn't really up, just a few rollers, but that's all I felt up to this morning.

In and out, in and out—I caught a couple of good ones, but my heart wasn't in it. It was early, and I was sure that Leslie was still asleep, so I rode in past the reef and rolled off the board and then climbed back on, lying flat on my back and looking up at the sky.

I felt the sun right down into my bones, warm and pleasant. When it got too hot, I dropped my hand in the water and splashed the cool Pacific over me. I closed my eyes. It was better than a steam bath.

Jerry would have liked this.

Don't think about that.

Okay.

Too late.

All right, God damn it all to hell.

Death is oblivion and life is a warm sun and drifting in the water inside the reef at Ala Moana and the only rain is miles away, over the Pali cliffs, over there.

Rain and weather, weather and snow, snow and cold, cold and Korea, Korea and Panmunjom. You could make a little jingle out of it.

Panmunjom.

The lovely thing about Panmunjom was that it was in the neutral corridor. Nobody shot at you in there, in the neutral corridor, because the opposing forces allegedly were negotiating peace and it would have been bad form to shoot a delegate to the armistice talks. It was more than just luxury to be there; it was like closing the door in death's face.

Panmunjom was just north of Munsan-ni and the railhead where the press train was parked, more or less permanently. Correspondents lived on the train in relative luxury (relative to the way they lived in the field, under fire and sleeping in the snow). In one direction and close by was "E" Medical Company, Easy Med, where you could count on getting fixed up if you became *hors de combat*, unless you were one of the many corpses stacked like a cord of wood outside the tents, stiff in the cold. In another direction and nearby was Munsan-ni.

If you drove north of Seoul for about two hours on the road that the raiders of Genghis Khan took on their plundering foray into Chosen, you came to an apple orchard. There the road forked twice and then branched off into six or seven roads. But if you turned right again and crossed a little stream, it put you in the orchard at Munsan-ni and you were in the middle of the United Nations Command (Advance) camp. Here the delegates to the truce talks lived, ate their meals, read their mail from home.

Several hundred men were stationed there, cooks and guards and clerks. The interpreters and stenographers lived there, and the Navy's Combat Camera Group operated out of Tent Seven. They were among the finest photographers in the world, and certainly among the hardest drinkers.

By day you could hear the rumble of artillery in the surrounding hills, and by night you could still hear it but also see the flickering lights from the guns, like lightning on a summer evening. In the early morning there was that strange and unexplained pause that gave Korea its other name: the land of the morning calm. It never lasted very long, that period of freshness; then the day began and all hell broke loose somewhere and the delegates to the peace talks got into their helicopters to go to Panmunjom and meet with Nam Il and Kim Il Sung and Lee Sang Jo and the others from the other side.

Correspondents generally rode up in jeeps, swaying and bouncing along the snakelike dirt road. In summer the dust covered jeeps and men alike, a dry, white dust that got right down into your underwear. In winter the snow and ice made driving treacherous and the wind, born on some far Manchurian plain, whipped with a cutting edge through parkas and went knifing right into the bone. The ride took an hour and a half and was pure torture, but at least nobody shot at you.

The neutral corridor was clearly marked and inviolate. We would ride from Munsan-ni to Panmunjom in safety, if not in comfort, while outside the corridor on our left Navy Corsairs were plummeting down to make an air strike and outside to the right Marine Corps tanks were shelling Communist positions in the hills across the valley. It became a favorite harassing tactic of the Red delegates to accuse our side of violating the corridor's neutrality, but I had never seen it happen. Once they accused us of shooting up Kaesong, which was their base camp corresponding to our Munsan-ni, but since they were keeping some of our troops there as prisoners, it wasn't bloody likely we'd shoot at it. They even took us up there in jeeps to see the bullet holes in the walls of the huts, but anyone can fire a bullet and we weren't convinced.

The Communists were stalling; that became obvious after the first few weeks. They were trying to get at the conference table what they couldn't get militarily, but all the time they kept up the military end of it and a hell of a lot of people died long after the truce talks began. It was a frustrating and bitter lesson. We didn't know it at the time, but Korea was the beginning of the era of the "wars of national liberation" with all the accompanying terrorism and confusion. I saw our delegates age prematurely with the bitterness that came from trying to negotiate with an insincere opponent.

A lot of it rubbed off on the correspondents.

It didn't take us long to spot the tactics. Some said we knew what the Communist technique would be long before the delegates, but I don't know about that. I know it wasn't long before our copy was full of how the other side was deliberately thwarting peace efforts. But not a man among us knew the truce talks would drag on for weeks and months and, finally, years . . .

I turned over on the surfboard and looked at the beach. A few bikinis out early, but only a few, and the lifeguard had showed up at last. I lay on my stomach and let my arms dangle in the water. To hell with the sharks; they had no business inside the reef.

Panmunjom.

When it was drawing to an end, we all realized it, and things loosened up a little. That was when I met Malcolm Leigh.

He showed up one morning on the other side of the line, standing with a group of North Korean correspondents. They looked like they were waiting to be told what to write, but he looked like the whole thing was amusing him greatly, and when he caught sight of us, he walked over at once and introduced himself. Some of the U.N. correspondents walked away, and the INS man nearly belted him, but when things were calmed down, we realized we had a gold mine in Leigh.

After the second or third day—we didn't want to rush him—we started pumping him with questions about our guys in the prison camp at Kaesong, what they were wearing and eating and how they were getting along. He did the same and we told him all we knew about the prisoners the U.N. troops had taken. Only a few correspondents got involved in this, but I saw nothing wrong with it. Leigh was articulate and observant and as far as I know he never lied to us. We never lied to him.

Eventually we reached the point where we were getting more and better information out of him than we were getting from the delegates on either side. I'm sure he felt the same about us, because he showed up every day, tall and awkward among the short Korean and Chinese newsmen, and left them as soon as he could to get over to the line.

He was a blond man, in his middle or early thirties, and quite the suave Englishman. His accent told of good schools and the proper social level. I asked him once if he were rebelling against that particular class, but he pretended not to understand and I never brought it up again. He never talked much about himself.

Three or four of us would stand around smoking and asking him questions. He would make a great show out of reaching inside his quilted parka and pulling out Korean or Chinese cigarettes and smoking them, never accepting ours. When we got our answers, it was his turn. His questions were couched in Party terms and damned cleverly put. We were careful how we answered them. His answers, on the other hand, were brief and pointed. He had a good mind, quick and direct.

I suppose I knew him as well as anyone. We never got on a first-name basis, but we did reach the point where we discussed other things beside the war. By the time they started the repatriation of sick and wounded (they called it "Operation Little Switch," a prelude to the bigger "Operation Big Switch" that was to come later), Leigh and I felt we were on rather good terms.

I stayed on at Panmunjom until the first repatriation ended. I interviewed a few men from Prison Camp Five, up on the Yalu River, and then, at the suggestion of the bureau chief in Tokyo, stayed with a typical repatriated Marine through all the things that happened to him until he reached the States. By the time I got back to Korea, Leigh had gone and I never saw him again and couldn't remember when I thought of him last. Until last night.

Why had Leigh asked for me? I couldn't think of a good reason, except perhaps because we were polite to each other and I guess he came to trust me. Was that all? Was that enough?

I paddled ashore and stood under one of the cold outdoor showers, washing off the sand and salt water. The sun was getting higher and I figured Leslie would be up and around, probably wondering if I had run away in the night. After lashing the board on top of the battered Chevrolet, I got inside and drove out of the park and up toward Manoa. It was a fine, clear day and I would have been content if it weren't for Leslie—and them, whoever they were. I drove leisurely through the University of Hawaii campus, marveling again at the multiracial coeds, and a few minutes later parked at home. Starting up the steps, I glanced through the window just in time to see Leslie slipping on his jacket in the living room. It fit neatly over the shoulder holster and the gun under his left arm. Suddenly it wasn't such a fine day and I decided to skip breakfast, though the surfing earlier had made me hungry. I went in and said hello to him, and he sensed my mood.

"Getting to you, huh, chum?"

"Yes," I said. "But you look chipper enough, especially with all that iron hanging in your armpit."

He grinned. "Part of the wardrobe. I hate the damned thing."

"Listen," I said, "the old Leslie Trent we knew and loved would have shot himself in the foot with a cannon like that."

He laughed and for a moment the old cameraderie returned.

"How about some breakfast?" I asked.

"No thanks. I had coffee soon after you left. Found the pot in the kitchen. You're a tidy housekeeper."

"Well," I said, "what's the next step. What do we do now?"

"I'll brief you this morning. There are a few things we have to work out, then we're all set. After that it's up to you. We'll move as soon as you can get ready."

"We?"

"I'm going, too."

"Great," I said. "At least I'll have a traveling companion."

"Sorry. I'm going, too, but we're not traveling together."

"Oh, hell. All right. Incidentally, just where are we going?"

"Is your passport in shape?"

"Yes."

"Visas?"

I went into the bedroom and got out my passport. I still

had multiple-entry visas for Japan and Korea, and you didn't need visas for Thailand and Okinawa. I came out and showed the passport to Leslie.

"You'd better get a few more," he said.

"Where?"

"Hong Kong. The Philippines. Better get one for Taiwan and one for Singapore. You don't need one for Vietnam."

"So he isn't coming across the seventeenth parallel."

"That's about the only safe assumption you can make."

"Good. I'm sick of Vietnam."

"It's too risky for him. He could get shot by accident."

"Anywhere else they'd mean it, huh?"

Leslie didn't bother answering that one. He was thinking. "Look," he said. "How long will it take you? How soon can you get the visas and do whatever else you have to do and be able to get out of here?"

"A week. Ten days, maybe."

"Make it a week?"

"All right," I sighed. "I suppose you want me to get tourist visas?"

"Yes. It'll be faster. You'll go out as a free-lancer. Battlefields revisited and all that sort of thing."

"Okay," I said. "What about a briefing?"

"We'd better do that a bit later."

"What?"

"You might as well go out in all innocence. Better for security in case the opposite numbers are awake."

I felt a sudden chill. "What the hell does that mean?"

"Just go out as a tourist. I'll meet you there and brief you on the spot. Then you won't have to worry about it on the way over."

"No," I said. "What's that stuff about the opposite numbers?"

"Well," he said, "Michael, old boy. It's just possible they know that Leigh's coming over."

"God damn it——"

"Don't let it upset you, old boy," Leslie said. He looked sort of rake-hell and amused, but I wasn't feeling too good.

"Leslie, we've both been awfully lucky. You know that as well as I do. You don't knock around Asia and these half-ass wars without getting hurt sometime, and neither one of us has got it yet. And do you know why? Because we don't take chances. At least I don't, and you didn't until you got hung up with whatever cloak-and-dagger troop you're with. I'm not very inclined to take chances now. In fact, I'm getting more and more inclined to say to hell with it and call the whole thing off."

He sat down and crossed his long legs and looked up at me, his smile gone. "Leigh won't come out without your assurances he'll be decently treated. He wants obscurity. He wants to go to the States and get lost. We're going to help him. We're going to give him enough money to make him comfortable the rest of his life. In exchange for what he can tell us. But, Michael, he won't come out unless you meet him."

"Where is he now?"

"Peking."

"He's English. Why the hell doesn't he go to England?"

"He's too well known in England."

"Canada, then. Australia."

"He asked for the States, specifically. Just as he asked for you."

"And what if I decide not to do it?"

"You already said you would."

"What if I change my mind?"

Leslie looked pained. "Don't ask questions like that, Michael."

"I'm asking. What if I say the hell with it all?"

"We'd have to . . . remove you."

I looked at him coldly. "You're putting a strain on a long friendship. Just what does removing me mean? Shooting me?"

"Don't talk rot, Michael."

"Well, what does it mean?"

"Stashing you away somewhere for a few days."

"And what about Leigh?"

"We'd try to bluff it through. Send someone out that looks like you. Coach him as best we could and hope he could pull it off."

"Probably wouldn't work."

"Probably wouldn't."

"Then, I'm stuck with it."

"I'm afraid so, old boy."

There were a few moments of silence. I got up and walked to the window. "Look out there," I said bitterly. "Brilliant sun and a soft breeze. Surfers. Look at those mountains with the clouds sitting on them." I turned to him. "You know what my major concern here has been? Trying to decide where to surf in the mornings and where to go for dinner at night. That's the rough problems I've had for the past few months. Can you believe it?"

"Michael, I told you in the beginning I hated to do it to you."

"You hated it, but you did it all the same."

"Certainly."

"Why?"

"It was necessary."

I sat down slowly. "You mean you've found something more important than friendship?"

"That's the way it is, Michael."

"Then, I envy you," I said. "Or maybe I pity you. I've always felt nothing was more important than the way people feel about each other. No nation, no ideology, nothing."

"You're an idealist."

"And you're a realist, I suppose?"

"Michael," he said quietly, "we're in this because it's something that has to be done. We've been friends a long time. It would be a lot easier for both of us if we could go out there as friends."

In the silence I could hear the mynah birds on the lawn outside, raucous and bold. Somewhere in the distance there was a power mower going and a little farther off I could hear the faint noise of cars on a busy street.

"Okay," I said. "I'm not really angry with you. It was just so damned nice here while it lasted."

"You can come back to it," he said. "This operation shouldn't take very long. Then you can come back and go native."

"All right. I can be ready in a week. Where are we going?"

"You're a tourist," he said. "Don't you feel the itch to see Tokyo again? The Ginza, the sukiyaki, the geishas. Maybe a little side trip here and there, to Kyoto maybe, or Lake Biwa. Remember the boat we had on Lake Biwa?"

"And after that?"

"Seoul for a couple of days. Then maybe to Taipei to reminisce with old chums in the China Club."

"Go on," I said. "What's after that?"

"Hong Kong."

"And then?"

"That's all."

So Leigh was coming over in Hong Kong. "How will he do it?"

"I'll tell you later," Leslie said.

He stood up and for the first time I noticed his bag beside the couch. He saw me glance at it. "I've reservations at the Moana," he said. "You won't see me again for a few days. There's enough money on your bedroom desk to take you anywhere, first class. I'll mail you a ticket in a day or two. I'll be on the same plane, but remember we're strangers, at least until I give you the word. People in the East know we're friends, so there's no use faking it there. But until we get there, let's do it this way. Any questions?"

I shook my head. He thrust out his hand and we shook hands. "I'll be in touch with you," he said, "somewhere in Asia."

three

"HALLO, MR. HAWKINS, SAIR," SAID OLD Wu. "It is nice to see you again."

"Hello, Wu," I replied. *"Ne ho?"*

"Ho ma," he said, grinning. "You remember your Cantonese?"

"Only a little."

"How long will you be staying, Mr. Hawkins?"

"I don't know," I said casually. "I want to look around a bit. I'm free-lancing now, being a tourist most of the time. I have a little more time than when I was here last."

"Ah, I remember," said Old Wu, leaning on the counter. Outside the dust and noise of Taipei rolled against the walls in a familiar chaos.

". . . dangerous times," Wu was saying. "Was that the time you went over to Quemoy? Ah, I believe it was. Yes, it was, Mr. Hawkins."

"You have a good memory, Wu."

"It was because of the crash I remember, Mr. Hawkins."

Yes, the crash. We had walked out of here one morning at dawn and clambered aboard a C-47 that belonged to the Chinese Nationalist Air Force. The flight to Quemoy was uneventful until the last few miles, when we dropped low on the water to avoid the Communist radar on the mainland just across from Quemoy. As we leveled off above the water a Mig-17 came out of the sun and raked us once, in passing. The right engine caught fire and we burned all the way into Quemoy. When the pilot sat it down, the right engine dropped off and we careened down the matted airstrip. Every man in the cabin walked away alive but battered, though the pilot and copilot were killed. Instantly, somebody said. The copilot had been a distant relative of Wu's, and when I came off Quemoy a couple of weeks later, I sat in the bar with Wu for a long time, telling him how it happened.

"I'll have your bags put in your room, Mr. Hawkins," Wu said. "Why don't you go in the bar and relax. You know the China Club always buys the first one."

"Yes. I know."

I pushed through the heavy doors and stepped into the bar. It was a real bar, deep seats, a long Philippine mahogany bar and the walls a subdued red. There were several familiar fixtures—the models of the Chinese junks, the chandeliers, and the Chinese bartender that everybody had called Spike for so long nobody remembered his real name.

"Hello, Spike," I said. "How about a brandy and soda?"

When he grinned, his face looked like it had been slashed with a knife. "Can do, Mr. Hawkins. Nice to see you again." He went away and came back with the drink and I eased into one of the nearby chairs.

"Who's here, Spike?" I asked. I was the only other person in the bar at the moment. "Anything going on?"

He rubbed the bar slowly with a cloth. "Very quiet lately, but maybe things will pick up," he said. "A few people drifting in now. Roy Anderson of the AP is here. That crazy Frenchman is here, the Agence France-Presse man. Let's see ... oh, Leslie Trent is here. I suppose you knew that already."

"No," I said. "Wonder what he's working on here?"

"I heard he retired," Spike said.

"Oh?"

"Sure. Told Old Wu he came into some money. Just going where he wants to now, I guess."

I finished the drink and walked back out into the lobby and over to the desk and called to Old Wu. "I heard Leslie Trent's here," I said. "What's his room number?"

"Ah, Mr. Hawkins. Very sorry. You are his very good friend. I forgot to tell you he was here. He is in room six down the hall past the barber shop. But he has gone out now."

"Did he say when he'd be back?"

"Ah, no, sair."

I nodded my thanks and walked over to the door and looked out on the square. On impulse, I stepped out the door and started walking down the street to the right.

A lot of the noise in the street came from the pedicab drivers, who would pedal you anywhere on the island for practically nothing but who annoyed you constantly if you insisted on walking. But I insisted. I wanted to see what had happened to Taipei in the last two or three years.

Surprisingly, very little had happened to Taipei. They were knocking down buildings and putting up new ones, like every place else in Asia, but the new buildings were very similar to the old, so you got the feeling of continuity, of life and death but humanity going on somehow. It's very easy to get that feeling in China.

Much of the dust was caused by the construction. It fell on everything and everyone, and on the food in the open-air markets. I crossed the trolley tracks and turned left. There under the elevated railroad was the restaurant with Szechwan cooking, very hot and spicy. It was very dirty in there. It also was one of the best restaurants in Asia. I was feeling a little better about being back in Asia and I hoped it would last until I left again.

I walked around for about an hour, then returned to the club, known all over the Orient mainly by its initials, the C.C. It was a hell of a place. At one time all of the roomboys were in Chiang Kai-shek's intelligence apparat and one correspondent told me his place was so crudely bugged that when he lifted a picture from the walls, to see what had caused the plaster to crack, a bloody big microphone was hanging there. His reaction was to put the picture back carefully, then tell an imaginary companion a wild tale about how he planned to assassinate Chiang by sending him a bomb shaped like a pineapple. The next day the microphone was gone.

But I liked the C.C. and now, pushing into it again, I decided to swing into the bar for a predinner drink. For a while I had forgotten Leslie, but when I stepped into the bar, he was there.

"Michael!" he shouted, waving one arm.

"Leslie!" I felt like a ham actor.

"Have a drink," he said. "When did you get in? How long will you be here?" And for a while we went through the routine of Old Asia Hands whose paths crossed in a bar, a not uncommon occurrence for Old Asia Hands.

When the bartender went for a refill, I turned to Leslie and whispered, "All right, Peter Lawford. Is this Academy Award performance going to continue? There's nobody here but you and me and Spike. You want to brief me now?"

He grinned and shook his head. "Later."

"Maybe the rooms are still bugged."

"Maybe."

"Where, then?"

"We'll go out to dinner. Pick out a bar and drop in there. Nobody can bug all the bars in Taipei." He was right about that.

We talked for a while, drawing Spike into the conversation. After a bit a couple of men we didn't know came in. Spike said they were correspondents, new in the area. We asked them to join us and for a leisurely late-afternoon time we drank and talked. They were new and young and enthusiastic and once I caught Leslie's eye and smiled. He knew what I was thinking: it was the way we were once. All three of us, Jerry and Leslie and I, all that way once. And look at us now. Jerry was dead. Leslie had become a spook for somebody—I still had to find out who they were—and I had gotten out of Asia forever. Well, almost. It got to be damned depressing, finally, watching their eager faces, watching them try to appear blasé. I got fed up with their opinions, too. They were so damned sure of themselves. I was relieved when we finally broke it up and left the bar.

Leslie and I grabbed a large pedicab in front of the C.C.

"Where to for dinner, Michael?"

"I know just the place."

"Not that bloody restaurant under the railroad."

"That's it."

"I'll get dysentery again," he said gloomily.

"Good," I said. "Just remember who insisted on this trip. We could be dining in Waikiki."

"You bastard."

"Oh, you mustn't worry about me, Leslie. I've got a cast-iron stomach."

"I know that, you ruddy bastard. It's me I'm worrying about."

Dinner was very fine, especially the roast duck. I ate all of my food and a good bit of Leslie's. When we finished, I noticed the restaurant manager staring at us. I opened my mouth and belched and the manager smiled. Old Chinese custom.

Out in the streets again the night was warm and filled with flickering lights and the smell of charcoal fires, and stirring with the press of humanity. Taipei is not glamorous at night, not even pretty. It does have a strange sort of appeal, quite unlike Saigon's bustle or Tokyo's urbanity. Here the people seemed a little less sophisticated, which somehow made them more likable. We walked around for a while, then got into two separate pedicabs. Leslie was in front and I told my driver to follow him. In ten minutes we were somewhere deep in Taipei and a few minutes later Leslie picked the bar and we paid the drivers and went in.

It was noisy and crowded. It was ideal. No one would bother the foreign devils here and even if anyone spoke English, he'd have to be sitting practically in our laps to hear. I ordered a tall beer, Leslie the usual gin-tonic.

"Well, Leslie, you're on," I said.

"Righto. First I'll give you a little history."

"Okay."

He took a deep breath and started: "The Red Chinese hierarchy is complex as hell. So is their espionage system. Their main problem is that they've got a bureaucracy going and they haven't figured out what to do about it. There's a foreign espionage section under Foreign Minister Chen Yi and a military intelligence organization under Lin Piao, their defense minister. Then there's Hsieh Fu-Chih, who is Minister of Public Security, which is an intelligence setup, and there's the Social Affairs Department, which is really an intelligence unit of the Communist party. There's an executive arm of the Politburo headed by Teng Hsiao-peng, the secretary-general; it may be an intelligence or counterintelligence outfit. They've got spies in their embassies, in their trade and cultural and economic delegations. Then they've got free-lance agents and agents among the overseas Chinese. They operate a few overseas spy schools; we know where they are.

"Then there's the Hsinhua, the New China News Agency. It's supposed to be their version of the Associated Press or United Press International. Or Reuters, if you don't mind a bit of chauvinism.

"The Hsinhua has more than twenty bureaus overseas. We're pretty sure that every reporter in every bureau is an agent. It's a pretty good cover. A newsman can ask questions and nobody thinks its unusual. It's his job. So the Hsinhua types ask questions. Sometimes they get answers.

"Now, one of the things that would help us considerably is to know who's talking to the Hsinhua. We know that the so-called reporters are filing reports and, knowing the Chinese way of doing things, they're damned detailed ones. If we can get the names of Hsinhua's contacts, we can put the screws on them, make double agents of them and tell Hsinhua what we want the Red Chinese to know. The Hsinhua would be a major coup and we want it badly. Let's order another."

I signaled for two more and we sat silently as they were brought and paid for. I sipped the beer and looked at Leslie. You never really know anyone. Except for Honolulu, the last time I had seen Leslie was in Singapore and he had just beaten me by an hour on a story about the rioting, then had taken me over to Raffles for a consolation drink. Never in a hundred years would I figure him to become a spook. Yet here we were.

"You're daydreaming," he said.

"Sorry. No. It isn't that. Go on."

"Have to digress a bit here. Malcolm Leigh went to Korea as a reporter for the *Daily Worker*. His copy started showing up in *L'Humanité* and some of the other top Communist newspapers around the world. He was an excellent writer; I don't know if you've ever read his stuff."

"No," I said.

"Had a good background. Good schools in England and Switzerland. Good in languages. Leaning left all his life, young rebel and all that sort of thing. He was locked up a couple of times for mild acts of protest, but his father bailed him out. Very well known family. Korea was his big chance, his chance to act and write and he jumped at it. You met him there at Panmunjom. I hate to admit it, but the copy he filed out of Korea was as good or better than anything written from our side, if you look at it purely from a writing standpoint.

"He stayed on in China. He was so good he became a sort of embarrassment to the Red Chinese. At first they tried showing him off, parading him in front of the world to show he was a cultured and educated Englishman who chose communism. He got tired of it about the same time they figured nobody gave a damn, and they mutually agreed that he should hold down a job. The Hsinhua was a natural place for him, and he started climbing in it. Sometime—we think it was spring or summer of 1955—they sent him to an espionage school in Peking and when he came out, he was an analyst."

"A what?"

"Analyst. He was too bright to be an ordinary agent. They decided to make an Intelligence Analyst—evaluator, if you like—out of him. For years he sat at a desk in Peking. Hsinhua agents poured in reports and he sifted them, evaluating and making recommendations. To our regret, he was very good. So good, in fact, he's been moved right into the front office with Hsinhua's chief, Wu Leng-hsi. As the second-ranking man there, he has considerable influence with the Politburo members. He has become a very important person. He could tell us a hell of a lot. He is probably the highest-ranking non-Chinese in the government, and he isn't very damned far below the level of Mao Tse-tung and Chou En-lai and the others."

"You weren't kidding when you said he was a wheel."

"Not a bit of it, old boy."

"And now he wants to come out."

"Yes."

"Why?"

"He's frightened."

"Frightened?"

"He's learned too much. He knows too much. And he's starting to get the feeling that the top brass consider him a threat and he knows all too well what happens to people who become too dangerous, or even too suspect."

"Well, it's as good a reason as any."

"There's one more."

"What's that?"

"He's fallen in love. He's in love with a Chinese woman whose parents were killed by the Communists because they owned a little land and were, therefore, capitalists."

"I don't understand, Leslie. How is his getting out going to help her any?"

He looked at me and this time the grin was a little sheepish. "He's bringing her out with him," he said.

"For Christ's sake," I whispered furiously. "Are there any others I don't know about?"

"Take it easy, Michael. It doesn't complicate things any."

"Women always complicate things." I looked down at the beer in my glass. "What's her name?" I asked.

"Choy-lin. Chang Choy-lin. She's quite pretty."

"Damn," I said. "Damn."

But there wasn't time to protest further; I caught Leslie's sudden glance over my shoulder and I looked around to see two Chinese army officers weaving among the crowded tables, unmistakably in our direction. I shot a questioning glance back at Leslie and he shrugged "I don't know anything about it," he said. "Play it by ear, old boy."

The two officers walked up to the table. I started to rise but decided the hell with it. One of them, stolid and silent, stayed quietly to the rear of the small man, who stood looking coldly down at us.

"Mr. Hawkins and Mr. Trent, I believe?" His English was unaccented and clear. He wore the rank of captain. "I am Captain Fong. I am so sorry to disturb you." He didn't look sorry at all.

"What can we do for you, Captain?" asked Leslie.

"I wonder if I could trouble you gentlemen to come with me back to the China Club?"

"What for?" I asked.

"There seems to have been an incident. We believe you can help us."

"What sort of incident?"

The captain turned his black eyes briefly on Leslie, then stared into mine. "A man is dead," he said. "In your room. If you would be so kind as to come back to the C.C. with me, perhaps we can clear it all up without having to go down to headquarters."

"What man? What was he doing in my room?"

"Ah, we hoped you might tell us," the captain said.

"I'm afraid I can't help at all," I said. "I've been out with Mr. Trent here all evening. I'm sure I don't know the man at all."

"Oh, yes, you know him, sir. You know him as Old Wu."

There was a pause and the warning buzzer in the back of my head. I glanced at Leslie, but he was staring at the captain. "Are you a policeman?" Leslie asked.

"In a way," the captain answered. "Republic of China, Military Criminal Investigation Division."

"Why are you involved in this?" I asked. "Why not the police?"

Captain Fong smiled coldly at me. "The man you knew as Old Wu was Lieutenant-Colonel Wu of C.I.D. Shall we go, gentlemen? People are beginning to stare."

We got up and moved toward the door. Outside, as we climbed into a waiting staff car, I turned to Captain Fong.

"How did he die?" I asked.

"He was murdered," said the captain.

It was ironic. A murder in the C.C., occupied chiefly by correspondents and not one of them in sight when we entered the corridor and walked, Captain Fong leading, hurriedly toward my room. Outside my door were a couple of soldiers whom I assumed to be C.I.D. types. When they saw us coming, one of them opened the door and nodded to Captain Fong, and we all went inside.

I stopped and stared in horror at what had been Old Wu.

He lay between the bed and the desk, his dead eyes open and his mouth contorted, as if he had been screaming when he died. From him, twisting out in radial lines across the wooden floor, rivulets of blood lay dark red in the glaring overhead light. His head was smashed.

But what was so terrible was what had happened to him before he died. His right hand was a crushed and twisted mess; the fingers had been broken and all the nails were gone and it looked as if perhaps the wristbone was broken also. His shirt had been torn off and his chest was a mass of raw flesh, obviously scraped with a dull, cutting instrument. Then I saw the dull wet stain covering his groin and down the insides of his thighs.

Sickened, I turned to Captain Fong. He was lighting a

cigarette. "All right," I said. "I've seen it. Now what do you want?"

But he wasn't going to be hurried. He blew out the cigarette smoke in a long, calm line, then walked over and looked down at Old Wu again before he spoke. "How long did you know him?"

"Eight or nine years," I said. "Off and on."

"How often did you see him?"

"I used to get in here about twice a year."

"Did you know he was in C.I.D.?"

"Of course not."

"It is not so silly a question as you may think, Mr. Hawkins."

I didn't say anything to that.

"Did you have any special dealings with him? I mean, did you have any relationship other than your roles as a correspondent and Colonel Wu as a desk clerk here?"

"Yes," I said, and enjoyed the way Captain Fong momentarily lost his composure.

"Explain, please."

I told him about the trip to Quemoy and about the crash of the plane and Wu's relative dying, and how I sat in the bar and told Wu about it.

"And that's all?"

"That's all."

Fong turned to Leslie, who had been standing just inside the door. "And you, Mr. Trent?"

"I hardly knew him."

Fong stubbed out his cigarette and started pacing around the room, ignoring us. Once he stepped in one of the long, thin lines of blood and it irritated him. He scraped his boot on the floor distastefully. A moment later he turned abruptly and asked if I knew why it was my room that Wu had been killed in.

"Captain Fong," I said quietly enough, "I am just about up to here with you. If you want to make accusations, let's go to the police right now. Let's book me, charge me or whatever. If I'm under arrest, say so. Otherwise I've told you all *I* know, I don't know any more, and I'm getting pretty damned sick of you. You, personally."

"Take it easy, Michael," Leslie said softly.

Fong looked at me for a long moment. I met his eye and he suddenly broke into a grin. "Why, Mr. Hawkins. Of course we are not going to arrest you. You are completely free to go at any time. We merely asked your help in this unfortunate matter."

It was one of those dizzying reversals that seems to be typically Chinese, and I decided to use it.

"All right," I said. "I'm pulling out right now. How about a lift to the airport?"

One of the two men in the corridor stepped into the room and spoke hurriedly to Captain Fong. Fong turned to me again and said, "We are starting to attract attention. Perhaps we should get you out right away. I must thank you for your cooperation. If you would like to pack, Mr. Hawkins, we can take care of the checking-out arrangements."

I glanced at Leslie and caught a slight nod. "Fine," I said.

Fong turned and spoke to the guards at the door. Leslie leaned against the wall, smoking and looking bored. I carefully stepped over the blood and started packing. It didn't take very long.

"I'm ready," I said.

"I'll ride out with you," Leslie said. "If you don't mind, Captain Fong?"

There was only a very slight hesitation before Fong nodded politely, and we went out of the room and into the corridor.

"You've been checked out," Fong said.

"You're very efficient," I answered.

Outside, the night was warm and noisy. The car was parked to the left of the club, facing the square. The driver put my bags in the trunk and got into the front seat. Leslie and Captain Fong got into the back and the car pulled away from the club and headed toward the airport.

We reached the outskirts of the city. Captain Fong spoke to the driver a couple of times, but it was Mandarin and I couldn't follow it. Leslie was sitting quietly, his arms crossed, looking out the window.

I watched the lights flickering along the roadway as we hurtled by, picking up speed as we left the traffic of Taipei. My mind was racing, too. Everything had happened so fast, but it actually began, or so I felt, when I first arrived in Asia. There just didn't seem to be any end to violence or deception. Old Wu a lieutenant-colonel, C.I.D.; I wouldn't have believed it in a hundred years. Fong probably knew much,

much more and I turned in the seat to ask him about Old Wu.

As I turned I saw Leslie calmly ease the gun from his shoulder holster and point it straight at Captain Fong's chest. Fong was looking the other way, out the window.

"I say, Fong, old man, won't you stop the car, please?"

Fong's head jerked around and he looked into the muzzle of the gun. He had great control; there was no expression on his face at all and his voice was even as he ordered the driver to stop.

Leslie spoke again: "Michael, when the car stops, we're getting out. All of us. Stay out of the line of fire, but search the driver very carefully. Very carefully."

"All right," I said.

The land was flat and the driver eased the car off the road. Around us were rice paddies. There were no other cars on the road, and I realized, belatedly and stupidly, that somewhere we had gotten off the main road to the airport. We were still headed that way, but the driver had angled off onto a side road parallel with the airport road.

The driver switched off the ignition, keeping his hands well away from his body and watching Leslie in the rear view mirror. Leslie opened the door on his side and backed out of the car, then gestured with the gun toward Captain Fong. Fong slowly slid across the seat and got out the same side.

"Now you," Leslie said to the driver. The driver got out and Leslie motioned him over to where Fong was standing, still calm and expressionless. I got out and walked around the car and moved up behind the driver. The car lights were still burning, stabbing into the darkness and throwing off some light as we stood alongside.

I stepped closer to the driver and reached under his arms. There were no weapons there so I ran my hands down his sides. In the right pocket of his uniform blouse there was a small, flat automatic, a .22 or .25 caliber.

"Throw it away," said Leslie.

I turned and threw it overhand toward the nearest rice paddy. As I turned back, Fong leaped. He caught me completely by surprise. I felt him drive into my right side, knocking me into the driver. We hit the ground in a heap and I had sense enough to keep rolling. So did Fong.

Leslie's gun boomed and was followed by a scream of surprise and pain. I was on my feet again yelling Leslie's name at the top of my voice. In the darkness, with Fong going one way and me another, he couldn't have identified us.

"Get down, Michael," Leslie shouted and I dropped to the ground again. Leslie came up in the darkness, running low and then tumbling beside me. We lay there, breathing hard. In the dim light spilling off from the car's lights I could see a body crumpled on the ground, not moving.

There were two shots suddenly, very close together. The car's lights winked out and I could hear the falling glass as the sound of the shots died slowly in the still night.

I was getting used to the darkness and could see a little better. I turned my head to look at Leslie, but he was gone. He had moved away when Fong shot out the car lights.

I lay there trying to figure out what to do next. If I moved, I would become a target. If I stayed, Fong might find me before Leslie came back, and I was unarmed. Fong was nearby, but where?

The road and the fields were deserted. What might have been a farmer's house was off to my left, outlined against the sky but far away. No point in trying for that. I looked in the other direction. Nothing.

What happened then happened very fast, but I saw it clearly. Leslie had crawled around the car and reached up and opened the door. When he did, the dome light came on, and as it flashed into the darkness Leslie rolled to the right and came up crouching in front of the car. At the same time, Fong rose and fired from the right side of the car straight across the front seat and through the open door. The bullet's path was a good three feet to the left of Leslie and before Fong could fire again, Leslie shot him twice.

The bullets jolted Fong backward and he went down. As I got up and started toward him he rolled over on his stomach and tried to get to his feet.

"Stay back, Michael," Leslie warned.

Fong got up on his knees and elbows, his head hanging limply. He was coughing, a strange barking sound. Leslie squatted close to him and started to speak, but Fong suddenly collapsed and his breathing stopped.

Leslie turned him on his back again. Both shots had hit him in the left side of his chest, very close together. Quickly Leslie started going through Fong's pockets.

"Search the driver," he said, and I walked over to where

the driver lay, his face now merely a mask. In one pants pocket I found an extra clip for the pistol I had thrown away, and nothing else. "He's clean," I told Leslie, who was just standing up.

"So is Captain Fong, or whatever his name is."

"Leslie, I've got a hundred questions."

"I'll answer them on the way to the airport," he said. "It isn't far, and I want to get you out of town."

"All right. Do I hack on over to Hong Kong?"

"Right."

"What about the bodies?"

"Don't worry about them. Let's get started."

We got back into the car, Leslie behind the wheel and me sitting beside him in the front seat. I wasn't surprised to find my hands trembling and my mouth was still dry. No matter how many times you've seen it, death is something you don't get used to. Hardened to it, perhaps, but not casual about it.

Leslie started the car and we eased onto the road again, moving slowly because there were no lights. Leslie hunched forward and squinted into the darkness.

"I'm listening," I said.

"It's like this, Michael. They're good—the opposition—but they make mistakes, just as we do. In the first place, the Taiwan police would handle a murder, routinely. If there were international implications and the army got involved, they'd send at least a colonel. And if Wu were killed in your room the whole club would have heard it."

"How do you know?"

"Didn't you see how he was tortured? They were trying to get information out of him. They know something's in the wind, but they aren't sure what it is. They thought Wu might tell them, so they moved in on him. But they would have had to torture him elsewhere. They killed him someplace else and sneaked him into your room. Rather audacious, I must say. They stood there big as life in the club making no apparent attempt at concealment. Convincing, I thought."

"Christ, I was convinced all the way," I admitted. "What did they want with us?"

"I suspect they wanted to put us through the same mill poor Old Wu had gone through. Awfully sorry about him, Michael."

"Was he a lieutenant-colonel in the C.I.D.?"

"Of course not." Leslie smiled.

"I didn't think so."

"He worked for me."

"What?"

"He worked for me. Member of the outfit long before I got in."

I leaned against the door and peered through the windshield. We were getting close to the airport again; I could see its revolving beacon off to the right. I was beginning to feel a great letdown now. I wanted a drink and a good night's sleep and a few more answers, and I was beginning to feel depressed.

"Michael," Leslie said quietly, and I turned to look at him. "I know this is rough on you," he said. "Briefly, here's the way it shapes up. We're going to get Leigh and his girl friend out of China. The Red Chinese are going to try to stop us from doing it, only we have an advantage because they don't know what's afoot. They know something is, but they don't know what. Apparently my cover is blown and I guess yours, too. There's a certain amount of risk involved, but the results are worth it, if you happen to believe that our side is right and the Red Chinese are wrong. I believe that way. I think you do, too. Tonight you saw the opening round; I can't promise you it will be the last. I can't force you to go on, either, but if you don't, a lot of other people, possibly including Leigh and friend, are going to get hurt. You were selected because Leigh asked for you and because that minor-league job you did at Panmunjom proved you could keep quiet. That brings us up to this moment, and we'll be at the airport in a few minutes. Questions?"

"What do we do now?"

"Get you over to Hong Kong. I'll join you in a few days and we'll go up to New Territories and help Leigh get across."

"How?"

"The less you know, the safer you are. I'll tell you in Hong Kong."

"Where do I meet you?"

"Repulse Bay Hotel."

"Fine. When can I expect you?"

"A few days. There's some tidying up to do here. I've got to get rid of this car and see if I can get a reading on Fong. If I can find out who he works for—which Red Chinese agency—I might have a better idea of what to expect. And then I've got to see the right people and explain away Wu's body in your room and your sudden departure."

"Can you swing it all right?"

"Yes, but it will take a few days."

We turned off onto the short paved road leading to the terminal complex. Leslie stopped the car and turned off the ignition. "We'd better walk from here," he said, and we got out and opened the trunk and got out my luggage. We walked toward the terminal, only a hundred feet or so away. There were people around now, tourists with cameras and plane crews and the ground crewmen bustling around one of Civil Air Transport's jets.

Just before we walked up the terminal steps, I fired another question at Leslie. "Who do you work for, Leslie?" I asked.

"A set of initials," he said. "If I told you, it wouldn't mean a thing to you."

"American? English?"

"A joint command, Michael."

"You aren't going to give me the name."

"There's no need for it. You've heard of M.I. 6 and the C.I.A.—we're a sort of blend of them. Their agents work for us on occasion. We use a lot of different sources. Will that hold you?"

"I suppose it'll have to," I said, and grinned at him. I liked him in spite of the situation he'd gotten me into.

We went through the routine of booking me to Hong Kong. I had almost two hours to kill before I could get a Viscount to Hong Kong. Leslie couldn't afford that kind of time, so we shook hands and he walked quickly to the entrance and disappeared in the darkness outside.

I checked out and waited around the airport, a little nervously, until my flight was called. I got aboard gratefully and in a few minutes we were airborne.

I looked around the cabin of the aircraft; I don't know what I expected to see, but already I was enmeshed in some vast machine of deception and violence and murder. I didn't like it at all. I guess I was looking to see if I was being followed.

After a bit I relaxed and looked out the window. The stars looked close and brittle and I saw lights far below, probably from a large ship, maybe a liner taking happy tourists to Hong Kong. I'd be there myself before too long, and I had a moment of happy nostalgia for all the good times there and the friends and the pure hedonistic enjoyment of living very well very cheaply. I leaned back and thought of those times, stretching out the memories and smiling to myself.

When I awoke, the plane had started the descent into Kai Tak and I had one quick, lovely moment remembering the first time I had seen Asia, from this airport.

Then the engines died and I was down the ramp and seeing it again; the island was exploding with lights and sounds, new buildings shot upward into the soft night and closer at hand I could hear the musical Chinese voices calling, calling, all Asia wrapped in those infinitely varying tones, and out in the harbor, junks and sampans of the water people, always in motion. I felt pretty good about being back.

four

I WAS IN HONG KONG LESS THAN A DAY when an old wound opened: I answered the telephone and heard that soft, clear voice that once had moved my heart. She said, "Hello, Michael," and I suddenly went back five years to a time of love and pain.

"Hello, Lynn," I said.

"You don't sound surprised."

"I guess not." I paused. "I've missed you."

"We never lied to each other, Michael. You've been too busy to miss anyone. Remember?"

"Yes."

"Am I going to see you?"

"Of course. Do you still live in Kowloon?"

"No." She gave me an address on Queen's Road.

"I'll be there in an hour."

"Michael, don't ask for Lynn Cameron. It's Mrs. Lynn Bartlett."

"I see. I didn't know. My best wishes to you both."

"It's late for that. Lewis was killed nearly two years ago in Vietnam. I'm a widow."

"I'm sorry, Lynn."

"You may remember him. He came out from Sydney to work for the Australian Associated Press."

"I vaguely remember him, Lynn."

"Well, no matter now. I'm glad you're here and I'd love to see you, Michael."

"I'll see you shortly. Good-bye."

"Good-bye."

I placed the receiver back on the hook and sat staring out the window of the hotel. Lynn hadn't asked if I had married. She knew me too well. And I hadn't asked her how she knew I was back in Hong Kong. As a correspondent, she would have contacts at the airport and hotels, and I remembered she was good at her work. But, then, she didn't do anything badly.

I peeled and took a shower and thought about her.

Lynnette Cameron ... Bartlett. She was Eurasian, half-Scotch, half-Chinese. The first time I saw her was nearly five years before in Tokyo. It wasn't love at first sight; it took about ten minutes longer than that. We were at a press conference for some visiting American Navy brass in the Sanno Hotel. Most of the correspondents were watching Lynn, and I could understand it. She had perfect features, dark hair and eyes from her Chinese mother, but she had her father's tall frame and long legs. The press conference hadn't been over more than a few minutes before we were talking outside the Sanno and a half-hour later we were sitting in a quiet bar in the Nikkatsu, getting to know each other. In the days that followed I got to know her quite well.

Lynn was born in Hong Kong and grew up there except for a year in London. Her parents died when she was a child, but her canny Scotch father had left her enough money to keep her comfortable. Still, she worked. She started as a stringer for a big American news magazine, then wrote a book about China that got a fair amount of attention when it was published in London. By the time I met her she had become a correspondent for the *Daily Express* and was working on a second book.

I learned a lot about her in Tokyo. As a correspondent, she was good at her job, but she never forgot she was a woman. In her hotel room and mine she was uninhibited and passionate. In public she kept a cool reserve. It took a while for me to find out how insecure she really was.

Perhaps it was growing up without parents. Perhaps it was the sense of being Eurasian or just the comfortable society of Hong Kong, where she found a niche. I never found out for sure. By the time we were getting serious, I had learned that she wouldn't live anywhere but Hong Kong and she had learned that my job prevented me from living anywhere permanently. We might have worked it out somehow, but Laos suddenly turned into a shooting war and I had to leave. Lynn went back to Hong Kong and it was a year before I saw her again. We had written, off and on, and she was waiting for me at Kai Tak. We had nearly two weeks before I was sent to Manila to help cover an all-Asia foreign ministers' conference. In that two weeks we just couldn't make it go. She was afraid to leave permanently and travel with me, and there was no way I could stay in one place very long.

On the way over to her place I thought about Lewis Bartlett. He must have been based in Hong Kong on a more or less permanent status. I dimly remembered a tall, friendly Aussie. I wondered if she had loved him very much.

The taxi stopped in front of a gate flanked by two stone lions. I paid the driver and pushed open the gate and started up the walkway to a white house almost hidden in the trees. It must have cost a fortune to get this kind of privacy in Hong Kong. I stepped up on the veranda and a maid bowed me into the coolness of the living room before disappearing. I had time for one admiring glance around the room before I heard a soft footfall behind me.

She stood poised in front of the moon gate that led to the interior of the house, a tall, proud Eurasian beauty in a white cheong-sam, slit to the knee, and a jade pendant around her throat. The years had improved her looks and she must have known it, from the quiet confidence of her smile and the easy way in which she started to move toward me.

I met her halfway and put my arms around her and she clung to me for a moment before turning her lips to me. When we kissed, the years dropped away and nothing in them seemed to have mattered very much. I felt her stir in my arms and then she put her head against my chest and held onto me for a long time without speaking. Finally I held her at arms' length. "You're more beautiful than ever, Lynn," I said.

"I'm so happy to see you, Michael. You just don't know how wonderful it is to be with you again."

"You haven't changed."

"Neither have you."

We sat in silence for a few moments. There seemed so little to say. Finally she got up and walked to the interior of the house, calling for the maid. Then she was back with drinks and small talk and for the next hour we talked about friends and stories we had filed and events in Asia—the usual talk between correspondents who haven't see each other for a while. She told me about Lewis Bartlett. She didn't say so, but I gathered she had married him soon after I had left her for Manila, that last time when we had failed to reach an understanding. Bartlett was killed on patrol with the American Navy in the My Tho River, hit by a sniper as he stood on deck of the small patrol boat. I told her all I knew about Jerry's death, which she had known about, and there didn't seem to be much else to say. As we sat there in the cool house, with the hot afternoon sun beating down outside, a strange thing happened, a sort of electricity between us. She looked deep into my eyes and read them right: I wanted her, and I knew she felt this moment, too. I reached for her and she came into my arms, but when we had kissed again, she whispered, "Later." To clear my mind I walked to the window and stood looking out on the grounds around her house and the traffic in the streets beyond. I had kept her buried for years, not daring to bring her out of my heart and look at her. When I turned around to look at her again, she was smiling, very cool and lovely, but there was a promise in her smile.

"We've time," she said, "and you always liked Hong Kong. Let's enjoy it ... while you're here." She shook her head. "I'm not even going to ask you how long you're staying or where you're going. I just want to enjoy having you here, Michael."

"Then, let's look the place over again," I said.

A short time later we were walking in Wan Chai.

It was like sailing through a sea of Chinese faces, sounds, colors, smells. We got out of the cab on Fenwick Street and turned on Gloucester Road, walking out toward North Point. The trolleys loomed up and slid by like ships without sails and the policeman at the Tonnoch Road intersection did a graceful ballet as he guided the traffic by, his white-gloved hands arcing through the humid air, in command of the bedlam on all sides. Amahs hurried by, shepherding the offspring of the rich; a ragpicker lazed along, his eyes betraying him as an opium smoker; a giant sailor lumbered by, a Norwegian or Swede, carrying his seaman's clasp knife on a key ring and a seabag on his shoulder, and his eyes, like the eyes of all sailors ashore, constantly turned to the sea.

Off to the right was the old Luk Kwok Hotel, a Wan Chai landmark. To the left and a mile across the anchorage a liner was easing alongside a pier in Kowloon. I stopped to watch, then turned back and looked up toward Victoria Peak and let the musical names of Hong Kong ping gently through my mind: Des Voeux, Connaught Road, D'Aguilar Street, Dragon Road, Tiger Balm Gardens, Waterloo, Chatham, Fu House, and on and on.

We had set out to do the things I liked in Hong Kong, and after Wan Chai we took a tram up Victoria Peak and got off to see the old Correspondents' Club. Lynn had warned me it wasn't used anymore. They had lost their lease on the site and the landlord had refused to renew it, and the proud old building was falling victim to vandals. Most of the windows were smashed and there were scorched places on the terrace where fires had been started and stopped. I walked over to the edge of the grounds and looked over the crumbling stone wall and down on the city and the harbor, and beyond to Kowloon and the New Territories. Kowloon is a Chinese word meaning seven dragons, but the real dragon lay beyond those mountains to the north, and its shadow fell across all Asia. Lynn and I walked arm in arm back to the tram station.

Down from the peak we rented a car and Lynn took me on a tour of the island, a quick drive around Aberdeen and Deep Water Bay and Shek O Beach, coming back into North Point and then back into the city. We stopped in the new Hilton for a drink, and by that time I was starting to unwind.

I dropped Lynn off at her house, arranging to meet for dinner, and rode happy and surrounded by the thought of her back to the hotel on Repulse Bay.

I went up the steps and through the large lobby. My room key was still in my pocket so I went straight up the stairs to the second floor and down to my room. I unlocked the door, stepped into the dark room and switched on the light.

The gun was large and steady and aimed at my chest. Behind it a tall Oriental with wide, level eyes was watching me carefully. "Close the door with your foot quietly," he said. "Then sit over there. No noise, please." The gun never wavered.

I eased the door shut and walked over to the chair. I started to sit down, but his voice stopped me.

"First let me see your wallet. Be very careful."

I took my wallet out slowly and held it out to him.

"On the floor," he ordered. "To your left."

I tossed the wallet on the floor and he picked it up, not bending for it but squatting with the gun on me all the time.

"You may sit down," he said.

I sat in the chair and watched him go through the wallet. He peered at each card in it, glancing frequently at me across the ten or twelve feet separating us. He looked for a long time at my old press card and at my Hawaii driver's license. Only the press card had a photo and he looked longest at this. He didn't bother with the money, and he didn't speak again while he was going through the wallet. Finally he put the cards back in the wallet and tossed it back to me.

"I suppose you really are Michael Hawkins," he said.

"Of course I am."

Suddenly he put the gun away inside his jacket. He gave me a wide, friendly smile and walked over with his hand outstretched. "Happy to know you, Mr. Hawkins," he said. "I'm Bill Kim. I work with Leslie."

Dazed, I stood and shook hands. "Why all the cloak and dagger?" I asked.

"Had to make sure you were genuine," he smiled. "Sit down and I'll tell you about it."

I sat down again and leaned back and looked at him. He was one of the tallest Orientals I had ever seen, and one of the handsomest. He looked like he might have come from North China.

"It's all right to talk here, Mr. Hawkins. I searched the room. No bugs."

"All right," I said. "Suppose you tell me what you know."

"Sure," he said easily. "After you caught the plane for here, Leslie got rid of the car and the bogus Captain Fong and the driver. Then he got in touch with my office and asked me to come over and give you a hand. He's going to be delayed for a few days. There was some difficulty back at the C.C. because of the murder, but Leslie got it cleaned up all right. There was additional difficulty with the Taiwanese police, but I went down to help and we took the inspector into the bar and all had a few whiskeys and it got straightened out."

To my surprise I heard the warning buzzer start up in the back of my head. "Where is Leslie now?" I asked.

"Still in Taipei. There's some sort of problem I don't know about—a need-to-know basis, you understand—but he should be along in a few days."

I looked across at the bland, handsome face and the wide eyes. There was something wrong.

"What do we do now?" I asked casually.

Kim crossed his legs and settled back in the chair. "I don't think there's anything we can do until Leslie turns up. My instructions were to get briefed by you and then make any advance preparation."

"Preparation for what?"

"Ah, that's for you to say, Mr. Hawkins. My job is just to help you in whatever way I can."

"Fine," I said. "I'm expecting a contact tomorrow. After that I'll be able to use you and give you a full briefing."

He swallowed the lie. "Very good, Mr. Hawkins. I shall be in touch with you."

"No," I said. "I'll contact you. Where can I find you."

He thought that over. I could see he didn't like it very much. "I think that is impossible," he said. "It would destroy my cover. Perhaps it is best if I come here again after you have seen your contact."

I pretended to be annoyed. "I have a few problems, too, Mr. Kim. Suppose we meet somewhere, as a compromise?"

"All right," he agreed.

"Where?"

"Hong Kong has eyes everywhere, Mr. Hawkins. But somewhere in Kowloon, perhaps. How about Castle Peak?"

"Okay," I said. "By the wall?"

He agreed and we set a time, two days away. He was getting ready to leave when I asked him the question that had been in the back of my mind for the past few minutes: "Kim, is Leslie drinking very much now? It was getting to be a problem, you know."

Kim didn't look at all startled. "No," he said. "He hardly touches the liquor anymore."

"I'm glad to hear that," I said. "He used to belt the Scotch pretty heavily."

"Yes," Kim said. "But not anymore."

We shook hands again and I walked him to the door.

"Be careful," I said, and he didn't notice the irony in my voice. "There are enemies everywhere."

"See you at Castle Peak," he answered, and moved away down the hall.

I watched him walk down the hall and round the corner toward the stairs, then I switched out the light and closed the door and started after him. Mr. Kim was as false as a three-dollar bill.

I went by the sleepy night manager and out into the street just in time to see a Vauxhall pulling away from the curb and heading west toward Aberdeen. Kim was at the wheel and I couldn't tell if anyone else was in the car. There was a taxi near the entrance. I climbed into the back seat. "Aberdeen," I said. I had no hopes of catching Kim, but at least I might spot his car again. It would be interesting to see where he went, whom he met.

We rolled around Deep Water Bay; there was plenty of traffic on the road, increasing as we neared Aberdeen. I didn't see the Vauxhall anywhere and in a few minutes we were in the center of Aberdeen. To the right were stores and shops and to the left hundreds of junks and sampans crowded against each other. It was very bright in the center of town and I ordered the driver on through before stopping him. I paid the driver and got out and walked back, trying to stay close to the shops and out of the center of the streets.

I walked through the town twice before I spotted the Vauxhall. It was parked on a side street in the shadows. I had an urge to search it but decided against it. It was parked in front of a fishing supply store; I couldn't read the Chinese letters, but I could tell from the supplies for sale behind the shuttered metal front of the shop. The shop itself was dark. I looked around; from the small cafe on the corner I could keep an eye on the car. Turning back, I went into the cafe and took a table in the shadows. It was not very crowded.

I was still on my first beer when the metal shutters suddenly parted and two men stepped out of the store. I drew back into the shadows as much as possible. One of the men was

Kim, the other an elderly Chinese man whom I'd never seen before. They stood beside the Vauxhall and talked quietly for a few minutes; then Kim got into the car and drove away toward Victoria. I hadn't been able to hear what they said, but at least I knew where Kim reported.

I waited until the Vauxhall had been gone for twenty minutes and the old Chinese man was back inside the darkened shop before I left the cafe and walked out to the main street to get a cab back to the Repulse Bay Hotel.

Lynn was wearing Thai silk and pearls when I picked her up for dinner. In a city of beautiful women she was still dazzling, and all heads turned in the restaurant as we were shown to a table. All through dinner we talked of small things, but now and then we simply ran out of words and sat looking at each other. Over brandy we just stopped talking and sat with our hands touching over the table, searching each other's face and knowing what we found.

"I didn't know I loved you so much," I said, and it came out a whisper.

She smiled and reached for her evening bag. "Michael," she said softly, "this is the time."

I paid the check and we stepped out into the night, holding hands and not giving a damn about anyone or anything else in the world. It was that way all the way back in the cab and into her house.

She went straight into her bedroom, not even glancing back; she knew I was there all right, with that old fire still passing between us. I never wanted a woman as much in my life, not even Lynn in the old days. She turned to face me and reached up and took off her pearls as I started out of my dinner jacket. She kicked off her shoes as I was getting out of my own, and the rest of the way we watched each other without embarrassment. The noise of the street was very faint, but it wouldn't have mattered in any case. The room was almost dark, but there was enough light to see her clearly. She slid out of the silk dress and stood in front of me wearing only her black bra and panties, and slowly she took them off. She had a look on her face that I remembered— commitment and love and pride in being a woman and a lot more, all mixed in together. Without haste she walked to the bed and threw back the sheets. I looked down at her, at the good breasts and great legs and the place where those legs joined. Calm now, and unhurried, I lay beside her in the still night, and we turned to each other in love. Her skin was cool and she stirred as I found her lips. I heard her moaning under my busy hands and then I felt her hands, too, exploring. All my senses became more acute. I could hear and see and feel and taste and the night seemed to glow with something beyond my experience. I felt Lynn writhing against me and rolled over on top of her, not sparing her, feeling very savage and masculine now as we rushed toward a place we had started for the moment I saw her again. And we reached it together, reached it with a great surge of love and power and relief from pain, and a great joy in our hearts, and love.

When it was over, we lay quietly in the darkness a long time before she whispered, "My God."

"Yes," I said. And again there was a long silence.

"You know," she said finally, "it's like the years had never been. Why do you suppose that is?"

"I don't know," I said lazily. "But I'm glad."

"It was this way in Tokyo, and later, when you came here. But we didn't have any right to expect it to last."

"No."

She peered at me in the darkness. "You're smiling."

"Hell, yes, woman. You don't know how good you are." I put my arms around her. "Or how much I love you."

She kissed me gently and pulled away. "What's the matter?" I asked.

"I don't think we should talk too much of love."

"Why not?"

"It hurts too much."

I tried to read her eyes in the darkness. I knew what she meant. "Maybe this time we can handle it better."

"I didn't ask you for any promises, Michael."

"And I'm not giving you any. I just think we have a better chance this time, that's all."

She looked at me curiously. "Why?"

I rolled over on my back and looked up at the ceiling. "Well, for one thing, I'm not knocking around Asia anymore. I'm going to settle in Honolulu and try to write. I've saved enough money over the years to keep me going for a while. I just don't want to kick around Asia for another twenty years with nothing to show for it but a few scars."

"Then, why are you back here now?"

"It's sort of a final tour. I'm gathering some material and taking a last look and then I'm going home for good."

"Do you mean that?" she whispered.

"With all my heart. And as far as I'm concerned it solves half of our problem. The rest is to convince you that Hong Kong isn't the world and that you could be happy with me in Hawaii."

She leaned over and kissed me again. "I could be happy with you anywhere."

I felt my heart pounding. "Then, how about it?"

She hesitated. "I'd want to think about it, Michael."

"All right. I won't rush you."

"Please, darling, don't sound so hurt. This is pretty sudden after not seeing you for years. I need a little time."

"I don't know how much time there is," I said, and my mind started to slip back to the past days and I wondered if Leslie were all right. I tried not to think about it. For an instant I wondered how Leslie would react if I said the hell with it, that Lynn and I were taking off for Hawaii and to hell with Malcolm Leigh. But I knew I wouldn't do that.

I turned and looked at her silhouette and listened to her quiet breathing. I put out my hand and ran it down her stomach and felt her move under my touch. Our kiss started gently but built to desire, and this time the lovemaking was longer and slower, but total. When we were still again, there was a great peacefulness in the room.

"I've got to tell you something, Lynn."

"Yes?"

"I need your trust."

"Of course."

"I'm not going to see you again for a while, maybe not until you come to me in Honolulu—if you do."

"All right," she said slowly. "I'm sure you have a reason."

"It's a good reason. I'm working on something and if I think about you very much, it isn't going to get done the way it should." I couldn't tell her that I had no idea when Leslie would turn up or what would happen then. And I couldn't tell her that if it got to be dangerous, I didn't want her involved.

She sensed something, though. "Look," she said, "I'm not going to press you on this. I understand. Let's just wait and see what happens."

"You're a marvelous girl," I said, and kissed her.

We lay with our hands touching and after a while we fell asleep. When I woke up, the sky was growing light.

I got up and dressed, watching her sleep. She was beautiful, even in sleep, and as I eased out of the bedroom I tried not to think about what life had been without her. Would she come to me in Honolulu? I didn't know, but there was hope.

I found a cab and started back through the early morning grayness, with Hong Kong coming alive on all sides. Out past the anchorage the water people were heading to sea. I sat back in the cab and thought of Lynn, how she had looked, and the lovemaking, and the promise of the future. It was going to be very hard to stay away from her the next few days, but I had to do it. Leslie would be arriving and maybe Leigh and maybe others. I didn't want Lynn with me if there was any danger. So I wouldn't see her again or even think about her until this was over.

It wouldn't be easy.

At the hotel I ordered breakfast on the terrace, watching the sails between the bay and Lamma Island. Mostly they were the faded red sails of fishing boats, but here and there were yachts out of Stanley or out of Hebe Haven on the Kowloon side, the white sails of the yawls and catboats gleaming against the backdrop of the green sea and the dark green outline of the nearby islands.

Piracy was born here. Castle Peak, where I was to meet Kim, was a notorious pirate harbor until not too many years ago, and the many hidden coves over on Lantau Island spawned pirates more vicious and cunning than anything ever seen in the Caribbean. Hundreds of junks existed for the sole purpose of piracy; hundreds more were innocent fishermen by day and pirate vessels by night. By moonlight the junks would push off the beaches of Lantau and Cheung Chau and raid the pearling fleets, occasionally getting bold enough to take on armed foreign vessels.

I shook the thoughts of pirates out of my head and tried to concentrate on Kim. I knew this: he worked for the other side, he knew something was going on, he expected to find out from me and hopefully before Leslie turned up, and he undoubtedly was having me watched. What I didn't know was what his next move would be or when he would make it. It seemed certain nothing would happen until our meeting at Castle Peak, although he might be a little suspicious when I failed to meet a "contact" before going to Castle Peak to see him. My only advantage was in knowing he was false. But how to take advantage of that? I wasn't cut out to be a damned spy, and I longed suddenly for Hawaii and a little peace and quiet. Things were moving too fast for me.

In the afternoon I went over to Kowloon again; I talked long and leisurely with cabdrivers, bartenders, store owners and waiters. If I were being tailed, I might as well give the opposition a chance to earn their money, and it might convince Kim I had made contact somewhere along the line. I wasn't sure what good this would do, but it seemed the thing to do at the time. Everywhere I went I kept an eye out for anyone following, but if I were tagged somewhere, they were good because I never saw anything or anyone suspicious. In midafternoon I had an impulse to buy a gun but couldn't figure out how to go about it. It was a strange feeling; in Hong Kong I could hire an assassin for roughly ten dollars in American money, but I couldn't buy a gun. I didn't want to run afoul of the British police and I was sure they would keep tabs on anyone buying a firearm in the colony.

Early in the evening I strolled down Nathan Road and turned into the Peninsula for a drink. I liked the Peninsula; it was old and Victorian and expensive, but it ran with the taut efficiency of a British man o'war, and it had the advantage of being close to the ferry docks. I had several drinks and listened to the Filipino band, with its sexy girl vocalist, then went out again and down to the ferry pier and crossed back over to the Hong Kong side.

It was on the ferry going back that I got my first shock of the day. I was sitting near the front on the upper deck when the old man came and sat across from me, his face in a three-quarter profile. He never glanced at me, but I knew what he was there for. It was the same man I had seen Kim talking with outside the fishing supply store the night before.

In a few moments we would be tying up at the pier by Connaught Road, and I decided, quickly, to see if I could confuse him. When the ferry bumped to a stop, I hurried down the gangplank and noted with satisfaction that the old man was right behind me. He was feeling pretty secure, not knowing I realized who he was. When we got to the bottom of the ramp, I swung around and got in the line of people going back across, bought my ticket for one Hong Kong dime, and walked back up the ramp on the same ferry. I had the satisfaction of seeing the old man torn by indecision, and while he hesitated the ramp was pulled in, the whistle shrilled, and we pushed off again for the Kowloon side, leaving him standing on the dock.

Probably they had tagged me all day; I had no way of knowing. If they followed up by tagging everyone I had talked to, they had plenty of work to do for the next day or so. At least I had caused them a little trouble. Certainly I had confounded the old man, for a while at least.

I took the ferry back again, not minding the extra trip. Riding the Star Ferry is one of the finest things you can do in Hong Kong. The view and the sunset seldom disappoint anyone, and they didn't this day. I drank it all in, enjoying myself immensely. The good feeling lasted all the way back to the hotel. I had a cooling bath, then called down for a paper and some beer. I switched on the overhead fan, adjusted it to the speed I wanted, and relaxed with the paper.

I found Leslie's obituary on the fourth page.

My eye ran over the head at first without paying attention. Then it registered and I felt the shock jolt through me.

The story was datelined Taipei. Yesterday, it said, a car had hurtled through a guard rail on the new road between Taipei and Kaohsiung, turning over and burning. One body was found, badly charred. From identification in the pocket, police determined the dead man was Leslie Trent, former Reuters correspondent and now a free-lance writer. The body was cremated and the ashes buried in Taipei because Trent apparently had no surviving relatives. Police said they could not explain what caused the car to go out of control. It was logged as an accidental death on police records.

My first reaction was disbelief. My second was anger.

Leslie was dead, all right. They had killed him.

I took it pretty hard. Jerry Ward was killed in a war. In a war you expected to get killed or hurt and then you hoped you wouldn't and went out and did your job. But Leslie was murdered. Even if it were a cold war, it still came out murder.

I read the story again. It didn't say anything about his dying instantly, but I'm sure that's what the police would have said to me. I thought about Leslie a long time before I got around to wondering what I should do next. My first inclination was to get the hell out, but that was impossible. Kim, and others, knew me. They'd stop me wherever I tried to go. There was some comfort in knowing that Leslie's friends knew about me, too, and if I stayed on long enough, one of them would contact me. But how could I tell if they were straight? Kim might have fooled me if he hadn't stupidly agreed when I mentioned Leslie's drinking Scotch.

I got up and walked around the room. I had the same gnawing in my stomach and the same dry, copper taste in my mouth that I'd gotten used to a long time ago. Now what, now what?

The telephone rang. I picked it up and said, "Hawkins."

"Kim here, Mr. Hawkins." He sounded depressed.

"Yes?"

"Have you seen the evening paper?"

"About Leslie, you mean? Yes."

"It's true. I checked with my office in Taipei."

I'll bet you did, you bastard, I thought, and had trouble keeping my anger out of my voice.

"What do we do now?" I asked.

"It's up to you," he said. "I suggest we keep to the plan we discussed previously. Tell me all you can tomorrow and we'll take it from there."

"You mean go ahead without Leslie."

"Yes."

Then, that was the game. They'd killed Leslie because he wouldn't talk or because he'd expose Kim here. Now they were relying on me to tell them what it was all about. They apparently had taken me at my word, believed me when I told Kim I'd learn everything from a contact and then pass it to them. We'd see about that.

"Hawkins?"

"Still here. Just thinking. I guess you're right. In the absence of any directives we might as well go ahead."

He did a good job of keeping the elation out of his voice.

"All right," he said. "You've made contact, then?"

I thought hurriedly. Why not? Nothing to lose.

"Yes," I lied. "Early today."

"Good," he said. "See you then. And, Hawkins . . ."

"Yes?"

"Very sorry about Leslie. Very sorry," and he rang off.

I almost slammed the receiver down on the son of a bitch.

I walked out and set the lock on the door. My hands were shaking and I could feel the pulse pounding behind my eyes. I walked downstairs and out on the terrace. A waiter took my order for a double Scotch and brought it to me at a table far out on the end of the terrace.

Lights were winking on as I drank and looked at the charming face of Asia. The fishing fleet was coming in and I could hear the cries of the sailors across the water, yelling from junk to junk, happy with a good day's catch. I could smell the pungent, sweet-sour odor of pork cooking over charcoal somewhere below the terrace, and behind me was the buzz of cocktail-hour conversation as the terrace began to fill up with tourists.

The other face of Asia was hidden, but it was there, all right; I knew it by the obituary in the evening paper, by the old man on the ferry, by Kim and all that he represented.

Which was the real Asia? Which the facade?

You could spend a lifetime there and never know the heart of Asia. You would know its mind, perhaps, its ambivalence, its poetic soul and pragmatic approach, its mysticism and rock-hard realities. You could never learn the heart of Asia.

But Asia would know you. It would find you out. And if you were strong, it would respect you, but if you were weak, it would destroy you.

No point in this, I thought, no point.

I gave it up and went back to my room and lay down in the darkness, looking up at the turning fan. Where had I seen one of those last? Dimly I remembered seeing one in a bar in Saigon, the day Jerry was killed. Oh, hell.

It was a long time before I fell asleep.

I was up early and had an early breakfast. I changed into gray British slacks and a blue sports coat, knotted a cravat, and took a cab into Victoria. In a little shop just off Queen's Road Central I bought a sheath knife that strapped snugly around my left forearm. If I couldn't get a gun, I meant to have some protection.

Back in Kowloon, I walked up Salisbury Road and found a car rental. I took one for the day, a battered, three-year-old Morris. I had a hell of a time getting it without the guide-chauffeur, but I managed. The engine seemed all right.

I headed northwest, past the Li Cheng Uk tomb and on through Tsuen Wan and into Tao Fong Shan, where the old Christian monastery sat disguised as a Chinese temple. I drove on past Kam Tin, the forbidden, walled village, and on to the Fanling Golf Club. I drove aimlessly for a while, then

stopped for lunch at a small, filthy restaurant in Lau Fau
Shan, eating oysters and watching the fishermen lugging their
catch to the market in the center of town. It was a fine, clear
day, humid as ever but with a slight breeze, and as evening
approached, the breeze picked up a little and I could see
whitecaps out in the shore swells as I headed south from Lau
Fau Shan and down toward Castle Peak.

I hadn't any definite plan in mind. I just wanted to see
Kim and see what I could learn. If it came down to the wire,
I meant to use the knife; the memory of Leslie was still
strong and I could feel the anger, as cold as the knife blade,
and as sharp. I had never killed a man; killing Kim wouldn't
cause me to lose any sleep, though, and if I had to, I would.

Castle Peak was a beacon in the old days, and a lookout
post. It was used by the Imperial Coast Guard to watch for
pirates. The idea was to spot the pirates from the lookout
and direct Coast Guard units to the scene of the action.
Many times the Coast Guard got on the scene too late, and
pirates had raided the pearling fleet and were standing hard
for the open sea by the time the Coast Guard arrived. The
pirates sold the pearls at other ports along the China coast or
traded them in Macao, just a few hours' sail away.

Even before the Coast Guard, the magnificent bay was
used by pirates as a base. Now it was the home of a good
many of the estimated 11,000 fishing boats in Hong Kong
waters.

I pulled the Morris off the road just before dusk and
walked up the rise toward the walls of the old castle. There
was a long moment when the sun started down, dropping like
a sinking ship, its rays shooting out and painting the sky to
the west. Then it was gone and the quick night of Asia
dropped, without any preliminaries, over both land and sea. I
looked at my watch and started walking.

The path became more narrow and the few tourists that
had been up to see the old landmark were gone. It was quiet
and calm and the stars were out, and the breeze was still
strong from the northeast. I could hear my shoes crunching
on the gravel path as I approached the castle and rounded
the corner on the ocean side.

Kim was already there, sitting on a rock and smoking a
cigarette. As I walked up he rose to meet me.

"Right on time," he said, and smiled. He looked calm and
confident and I felt the anger throbbing in me.

"Hello, Kim," I said, and loosened the knife in its sheath, a movement he didn't notice.

"Shall we sit?" he said, gesturing toward the boulders in front of the old wall.

We sat very near each other, he quiet and still, me with my heart hammering and a coldness in my stomach.

"Well," he said, "I'm sorry about Leslie Trent, but I suppose we have to carry on. Are you ready to brief me?"

"Sure," I said, and hit him hard under the right eye.

I put everything I had into it; he went off the rock and landed on his left side, heavily, and rolled onto his stomach. He was shaking his head and starting to get up when I kicked him hard in the side and he went down again. Before he could move, I put one knee in his back and held the knife at the back of his neck.

"The first one was for Leslie," I told him. "The second was for me."

He turned his head slowly to one side and coughed into the dirt. "What the hell is this all about?" he spat. I dug the knife point a little deeper into the back of his neck. "You're going to tell me, Kim," I said. "Or else."

He lay still for a moment. "We underestimated you, Mr. Hawkins," he said finally. "You are not an amateur after all, are you?"

It wasn't what he said that disturbed me; it was the easy way he talked with a knife at his throat.

"Never mind that," I growled. "Let's have an explanation and have it damned fast."

He chuckled. "You are an idiot, Mr. Hawkins," he said.

It was the last thing I heard him say for at least an hour. There was a sudden flash of pain and a great, rushing noise in my head and the whole world turned black.

Waking up was slow and painful. The back of my head was sore as hell and somebody kept rolling it from side to side. A few minutes later I realized I was on the floor and the floor was moving; I thought this over for a few minutes, then opened my eyes.

I looked straight up at a mast with a red sail straining under the wind, and beyond the end of the mast the stars were cold and brittle. I tried to move my arms, but they were tied behind me; my fingers were getting numb from the ropes around my wrist and elbows. My feet were tied at the ankles and when I tried to lift my knees, I knew they had tied my feet to something on deck. I was helpless and my head ached and I began to get more than a little scared. Trying to raise my head was no good. It just ached more, and I couldn't see anything anyway. I looked up at the stars and tried to think.

It was stupid of me not to consider that there would be more than one of them. Kim was an old hand at this sort of thing. Now the question was, where were they taking me and why?

Obviously I was in the stern of a junk, a large two-master. Like all junks, she felt seaworthy, but like all junks she was beamy and rolling in the sea. I could feel the wind on my right cheek and we seemed to be moving with the current, which would put us in a westerly direction. I could hear the crew moving about the deck, but I kept my eyes closed, listening.

I had decided we were on our way to Macao when the junk tacked south and the wind moved around to my left. There were footsteps toward me and I breathed naturally and kept my eyes shut and heard the footsteps going away again. West and south: that would put us beating either toward one of the islands, which was likely, or out into the open sea, which was possible but not likely. Finally I opened my eyes and tried to sit up. Kim loomed over me and grinned sourly down at me. I was pleased to see his right eye swollen almost shut.

"Be patient, Mr. Hawkins," he said, his voice controlled. "We shall have you ashore in a few minutes. I know how anxious you are to continue our conversation." Then he was gone.

A Chinese crewman walked past me carrying a lantern. There was a soft call and an answer and I could hear the surf breaking gently on the beach. The sails came down together and were furled expertly; this was a crew that sailed together often.

Kim and one of the crewmen came back to me. The crewman cut the rope around my ankles and they jerked me roughly to me feet. My head felt as if it were coming apart. I blinked and looked around. There were no lights except the lantern on the junk and one on the beach. Someone threw a plank over, one end on the junk, and Kim pushed me forward. I stumbled up to the plank.

"Move, move," Kim whispered. I teetered off-balance for a moment on the plank, then edged down it cautiously until I was on the beach, up to my sore ankles in the sand. Kim was right behind me, shoving, and I moved toward the lantern. It was held by an evil-looking Chinese, who stared at me.

"Hello, Fu Manchu," I said. It was all I could think of.

Kim clipped me across the neck with the edge of his hand, a sensation like getting hit with a length of pipe.

"Quiet," he said needlessly. I didn't feel like talking anymore.

We walked inland, the nasty-looking Chinese leading with the lantern, then me, followed by Kim and another man from the junk. As we moved off I could hear the plank being pulled in and the junk's sails going up again. They had a damned good crew there.

My night vision was getting better and I could see the outline of hills to my right. We were walking parallel to the beach but up past the foliage line and along a narrow path. I could see nothing on the seaward side, no lights, no ships. I looked curiously at the hills and beach. There were no landmarks that I recognized. It was strangely quiet.

Despite the breeze, I was perspiring, and not only from the rapid walk up the path. I was in a hell of a fix now and I knew it.

We walked for perhaps an hour, climbing gradually until we reached the point where I could see the white surf breaking far below. I still couldn't find any landmarks.

Abruptly the man with the lantern stopped. Before us was a large wooden shack. While I looked at it curiously two guards in the hills behind us walked up. One of them pushed open the door and motioned me inside and I went in followed by Kim and the others.

The light came from several lanterns swinging, ship-style, from the ceiling. The light gleamed on a number of automatic weapons propped casually against the walls and directly under the lanterns was a table around which sat four or five men, still holding cards. I took in the scene quickly and searched the room for another entrance, but there didn't seem to be one.

Kim spoke roughly in Cantonese, too fast for me to follow. One of the men reached for the pile of Hong Kong dollars in the center of the table and divided them evenly. They got up and moved against the walls. None of them had spoken, and the military-like precision with which they obeyed Kim wasn't lost on me.

"Sit down, Hawkins," he said, and I sat in the nearest chair, my back to the door, facing them.

"Like a drink, Hawkins?" Kim asked, as pleasantly as if we were in the Gloucester Lounge.

I nodded and a bottle and two glasses appeared. It was Scotch.

Kim spoke again and someone stepped behind me and cut the ropes. I sat rubbing my wrists and looking around the room while Kim poured a large drink in each glass.

In one corner of the room was a very good, very modern radio set. In the other corner were four bunks, tiered for maximum use of the space. Four bunks meant four men here probably round the clock. Rather expensive use of manpower, just to monitor a radio set. Kim's voice jerked me back to my own problem. "Drink up, Mr. Hawkins," he said. "It may help deaden the pain."

"Go to hell, Kim," I said meanly. "You'll get nothing out of me."

He laughed and it wasn't funny. He knew he'd get it out of me sooner or later and I had a sinking feeling he was right. He sat staring at me with what might have passed for amusement in anyone else.

"What makes you tick, Mr. Hawkins?" he asked, his voice still level and pleasant. "How did you happen to get into all of this? Somehow you don't seem the type for this line of work."

"I like surfing," I said. "I like women and Scotch and getting up in the mornings in Manoa and deciding where to go surfing. I like Sunday brunch at the Halekulani and dinner at Canlis——"

"Shut up!" His voice lashed at me. "You are not amusing. Stand up!" I stood up and he leaned across the table and gave me a short, savage chop with the edge of his hand. I felt like I had been kicked by a mule. It threw me off balance and I fell clumsily over a chair. Someone reached down and half-lifted me upright again. I could feel my nose starting to swell and the blood running down my cheek and around the corners of my mouth.

Kim smiled. "That is for this," he said, and pointed to his swollen right eye.

"Then, we're even," I croaked. "All right if I go home now?"

For a moment I thought he was going to hit me again.

Then he barked in Cantonese and two of them dragged me over against the rack of bunks and tied my hands, one hand to each side of the bunks and over my head. When they had finished, Kim walked over and slapped me twice, hard, then went back and took a sip of his drink. He sat at the table and looked at me for a moment and then came back and threw the rest of his drink in my face. I had time to close my eyes but not enough time to turn away, and the alcohol on my broken nose burned like a hot coal. It was all I could do to keep from screaming.

It was only the beginning. They worked in shifts; two of them on my chest and stomach, and then two coming back to slap me from side to side. The pain went right into the core of me, rushing in and vibrating and going out again to make room for new pain, from a different area. I passed out once and was barely conscious again when they started all over again.

Somewhere, in the middle of it, Kim's face was close to mine and he was saying quietly that I could end this unpleasantness by talking. I opened my mouth, but nothing came out. I didn't even have enough saliva to spit at him, but I tried. In a few seconds they started in on me again.

I was hanging by the ropes now; I couldn't stand any more, couldn't even think. My mind was whirling out of control, pushed by the pain in my body.

There was a sudden lull, a most welcome pause, and I tried to stop my spinning head and wish away the pain. It was very quiet because they were watching me die. The thought brought tears to my eyes, but they were gone again in a moment because I suddenly realized I had lost my mind. This was what it was like to go insane: you hear voices of dead friends. The voice belonged to Leslie and he was apologizing for being late.

With a great effort I forced my eyes open. The first thing I saw was every man in the room imitating me—they had their hands above their heads.

The next thing I saw was Leslie. He stood in the doorway with an automatic rifle in his arms. He was wearing fisherman's pants and a rough jersey and his face was scratched, but he was grinning and there was a light in his eyes.

I finally found my voice: "What kept you?"

The grin widened. "Sorry, Michael, old boy. Had a little

trouble outside. But it's all right now. Nothing to worry about."

"You've got plenty to worry about, Trent," Kim snarled.

"Leslie," I mumbled, "hell of a lot to tell you."

"Later, Michael. We're getting out of here. You've got to see a doctor."

"Take . . . Kim," I panted. I was getting awfully tired.

"Right."

"You're supposed to be dead," I said.

His answer was close to my ear. He was cutting me down. "Later, later. We've got to move out now."

I was free again, but I almost collapsed. Leslie put one arm around me and started moving for the door. I stumbled along shaking my head and trying to stop my head from spinning. I saw Leslie motion with the rifle and Kim started toward us.

"Watch him . . . Leslie," I said. "He's tricky."

We backed out the door into the night outside. Leslie lingered in the doorway. "Michael, can you handle a gun? Just for a moment?"

"Sure," I said. I'd do it somehow.

He shoved a pistol into my hand. "It's ready to go," he said. "Keep it on Kim. If there's any trouble, anywhere, shoot him first."

I brushed my sleeve across my face. The gun felt very good. "Okay," I said. "I hope there's trouble. The bastard."

"Listen," said Leslie. "I'm going to shoot up the radio. Don't worry about the first burst. If you hear anything after that, shoot him."

Kim and I sat on the ground outside, about twenty feet apart. The night was much cooler now and it helped. I could focus and I knew I could squeeze the trigger if necessary.

Leslie seemed to be gone a long time. I was getting a little nervous when I heard a short, sharp blast. A few minutes later Leslie came loping up. "Let's get started," he said.

"You'll never get off this island," Kim said quietly.

"Where the hell are we, Leslie?" I asked.

"Lantau Island. Tai O Town is down the beach that way," he said, gesturing. "We've got to stay out of there for now. Too many people and too many questions."

"Where are we going then?"

"Straight across the island, due east and right around the edge of this mountain. Shek Pik reservoir is up there to our left. If we strike straight across, we'll come up on the southeast side."

"And then what?"

"Steal a boat," he said, grinning. "This is where piracy began, remember?"

We started off and up the mountain, Kim in front with Leslie's gun on his back and me stumbling along behind. Once I fell and we stopped while Leslie helped me to my feet.

"The bastards," he said. "They'll pay for this, old boy."

I was beyond caring. Every step was torture, every yard a mile of pain. "I can't make it, Leslie," I said.

"Of course you can," he answered, and of course I kept plodding.

We were halfway up the mountainside before I remembered something. "Leslie," I whispered, "what about the others?"

"Locked in," he said. "I threw away their guns, shot up the radio. It'll take them a while to get out and once they do, they won't be able to find their guns."

"What will they do?"

"I don't think they'll try to run us down. Or if they do, they'll have to go into Tai O or the other way, north, to find a settlement where there may or may not be weapons. No, I think we're all right if we can just get off the island tonight."

"You can't win this," Kim said. It was the first time he'd spoken since we started hiking.

"Why not, Pak?" asked Leslie.

"His name's Kim," I said stupidly, through the pain.

"His name's Pak," Leslie said. "He's from Masan, South Korea, only he fought on the other side during the war and later managed to infiltrate South Korea's Naval Intelligence before he was discovered. He got out just ahead of the Naval Intelligence types and can't go back anymore. That's why he operates down here. He's good in languages. We've been watching him for some time."

"You son of a bitch," Kim-Pak said.

"I told you he was good in languages," said Leslie, and we kept hoofing it over the ridges.

Suddenly we were at the top. There were a couple of small islands off to the right and in the distance was Cheung Chau and Lamma Island and beyond that the lights of Hong Kong, showing us the way home.

"We're going to make it, Leslie," I said, believing it now for the first time.

"Not all of us, Hawkins," came Kim-Pak's voice, "not like this."

I turned to look at him. There was a curious light in his eyes and his lips were set. His handsome face looked suddenly more Oriental in the moonlight and he seemed at ease as we stood there on the crest of the ridge. He looked back at me for a moment, then turned his attention to Leslie.

"I'll make a deal with you, Trent," he said.

"I'll listen," Leslie replied.

"You tell me enough to satisfy my headquarters. I'll tell you enough. Then we part and let the fortunes of war decide the rest."

"Ridiculous," Leslie said.

"Not so ridiculous when you consider the alternative."

"I'll listen," Leslie said again.

"If you don't go along with the idea, you're going to have to shoot me here and now. Then you won't have learned anything."

"You're bluffing," Leslie said.

"No," he said. "Not at all."

I believed him. I don't know why. But I knew what was going to happen next and there was nothing to be done about it.

"No deal," said Leslie. "Let's get moving."

"Are you sure, Trent?" Kim-Pak said. "Absolutely sure?"

"Yes," said Leslie.

"Then, good-bye, gentlemen," he said, and calmly turned and started walking back down the path.

"Don't be a bloody fool," Leslie yelled.

The Oriental broke into a trot.

"Pak!" Leslie yelled.

The trot became a run. Leslie threw up the gun and fired. It was a short burst, but it was enough. The rounds knocked Kim-Pak off his feet and sent him tumbling. He lay face down and still. By the time we got to him, he was dead.

"Damn it," said Leslie.

"Jesus Christ," I whispered. No matter what side he was on, there was dedication for you. I wondered if I'd ever have courage like that. I doubted it.

We left him there; there was nothing else we could do.

"We've got to hustle now," Leslie said. "If any of his

playmates back there have gotten weapons by now, they may be behind us. They'll have heard the gunfire. Do you feel strong enough to step up the pace?"

"Yeah," I said, unsure.

Leslie wheeled and we started over the crest and down the other side, hurrying now. The moon was well up and we could see better and the breeze was still holding from the northeast, and most welcome on my battered face. It took us three hours, with frequent rest breaks, to get down the other side and to the shore. I collapsed in the bushes and stared up at the stars, panting. My nose had started to bleed again and every time we stopped to rest, I found a new pain.

"Wait here," Leslie whispered. He didn't have to say it twice.

In a half-hour he was back. "Let's go," he said.

"Hell, I said. "I'll never be able to move again. Where are we going?"

"I've got a junk waiting."

"How?"

"Money. They'll take us back with no questions asked."

"How do you know you can trust them?"

"They're impressed by the size of my wallet and the size of this machine pistol."

"Help me up."

We made our way down to the waterline and I saw the junk there, a small one, pulled up on the beach. There were four people on deck, one of them a woman, and all of them stared at my face as they helped me clamber aboard. Leslie came aboard. I walked back to the stern and lay down, terribly sore and tired. Minutes later I felt the junk go free of the beach and start out through the shore swells.

I don't remember much else about the trip back. I remember the gentle rolling of the junk and waking up once to find Leslie holding a wet cloth on my forehead, and heat returning—that was the sun coming up—and being helped into a car somewhere.

I woke up again in the emergency ward of a hospital; they had set the broken bone in my nose after giving me a painkiller. I don't know how Leslie did it, but he got me out of there and into my hotel room soon after that, without a word of it in the local papers. I spent the next day sleeping, waking up occasionally to see Leslie walking about the room or having a drink while he watched over me, and once I woke up to see him sleeping in the chair opposite me. He looked very tired, and I sympathized just before I fell asleep again.

I felt much better the next day. I woke up hungry and Leslie arranged for breakfast. He showered and shaved and changed clothes and I saw his luggage in one corner of the room. He had moved in with me. The hammering in my head was gone, and so was the pain in my nose. Now I was merely a mass of sores and aches, but they would go away in time. No permanent damage had been done.

"How is it," I asked Leslie, "you've miraculously risen from the dead?"

He sipped his tea and told me the story. He had gotten things cleaned up on Taiwan when he got word that the opposition knew about both of us. They were in a panic to find out what we were up to. They knew it was big, but they couldn't run it down. In desperation, they tried a gambit that almost worked. They planned to snatch Leslie in Taiwan and make me believe he was dead. By winning my confidence, they'd find out what we were doing. It almost worked, too. Leslie outsmarted them on Taiwan; the dead man belonged to them, but Leslie planted his identification on his would-be kidnapper. In Hong Kong it appeared the plan had worked, and Kim-Pak made contact with me. Leslie came over to watch them watching me, tailing both of us around town. He had one bad moment when they took me aboard the junk, though; with all the junks around Hong Kong he had trouble renting one to follow me, particularly to a deserted portion of Lantau Island. He got there a little late and had a hell of a time trailing us, to say nothing of having to surprise the guards outside the shack.

"I hope Leigh appreciates all this," I grumbled. "I hope to Christ he's worth it."

"He's worth it, all right," Leslie replied. "You can't know just how much he's worth it."

"I hope so," I said again and, surfeited with breakfast and a sense of security, promptly went back to sleep. It took two days to get me feeling reasonably normal, and in two days Leslie was ready to make his move, and finally, we gloated, the payoff was near.

We were in for a shock.

——————— five

"HAVE A LOOK," SAID LESLIE.

He dropped several photographs and documents on the table. I walked over and pulled a chair up to the table and sat beside Leslie, who had just returned to the hotel.

The first photograph was slightly out of focus and obviously shot in a dim light. It showed Malcolm Leigh and two Chinese beside a lake somewhere in China. They looked like they were on a holiday, but they still wore the universal garb of China, the pajamalike pants and strangely old-fashioned, high-necked shirts. There was a sampan on the lake behind them, barely visible. The photo had been taken late in the evening, apparently, and the three men in the picture didn't know they were being photographed. It wasn't a very good shot and I couldn't tell much about Leigh except the obvious things. He hadn't gotten fat, in fact looked very thin, and still had his hair. The rest of his face was in shadow.

The second photo was of a picture of one of the most beautiful women I have ever seen.

She was looking straight into the camera in a good light and the photographer had filled the frame with her image. What he caught was a woman in her early thirties, probably, who looked younger because of a flawless skin and a girlish, innocent smile. Her long hair fell forward across her shoulders and the wind had caught wisps of it and woven it gracefully across her neck at the moment the photographer had clicked the shutter. Her eyes were candid, almost whimsical. The whole effect was that of a pretty woman enjoying herself and entirely unaffected by the camera.

"I take it that's our Choy-lin."

"Righto," said Leslie. "Don't know where that was taken. The photo of Leigh and two pals from Hsinhua was taken just north of Peking at Mao's resort home. Leigh's been a frequent guest there."

I picked up the third and last photo. It was a clear shot of Leigh, much better than the other one. It was an oddly appealing picture. There was something about the eyes that aroused your sympathy. He was older, of course, and there were lines around his eyes, but it was the eyes themselves that drew your attention. They appeared, all at the same time, lost, amused, hurt, and determined. They were the eyes of a man who has suffered and loved and more than once pulled himself up by his own talent and drive. He looked a little like a reformed alcoholic. He hadn't changed much otherwise. There was the angular face I remembered from Panmunjom, a few lines in it now, and the hair thick and brushed straight back from a wide, low forehead. I couldn't tell from the photo if he'd gotten gray, but he'd changed very little otherwise, except for those compelling eyes.

Leslie sat down and pushed the thin stack of papers toward me. "Take a look," he said. "You might like to know what your boy's been up to the past fortnight."

The top paper was a reproduction of a commentary in a Peking newspaper, along with the English translation, under Leigh's byline. It was the standard diatribe about the U.S. in Vietnam, and I was a little disappointed in that it contained nothing original, not even a neat turn of phrase that I could admire. I said as much to Leslie.

"He's been following the Party line much more strongly the past few weeks," Leslie replied. "He's trying not to arouse any suspicion at all. It must be annoying hell out of him to have to write that nonsense when he could write much *better* nonsense."

I flipped through the other papers; they were much the same.

"Look," Leslie said. "Here is the sort of thing that put him a cut above the normal. This was written a couple of years ago."

I looked over the paper. It was a brilliant analysis of the forces that led to the founding of the Wei dynasty by the Toba clan of the Hsien Pei tribe in A.D. 439. It was a turbulent period in Chinese history, and Leigh's writing made it come alive. Then he tied it in to Mao and the Long March and China's upheaval in the 1930s. It was a damned fine job of research and writing and scholarship.

"Now," Leslie said, "if you can imagine being able to do this exceptional sort of work, then turning your back on it, as it were, and devoting your intelligence to espionage, then you can see why Leigh is valuable to them, and valuable to us."

"Yes, I see."

"And now in addition to that really fine mind and talent of his, he has the experience of information of some fifteen years behind the so-called Bamboo Curtain. It must be fascinating."

"You're practically salivating, aren't you?" I grinned at him. "Will you and I get to hear any of this, once he's delivered?"

"Of course not. Makes it damned frustrating, doesn't it?" And he grinned back.

"Leslie, if I hadn't seen you in action the past several days, I wouldn't have believed it. You sure you haven't been putting me on? I mean, it wouldn't surprise me if you'd been doing this undercover stuff for a hell of a lot longer than you'll admit."

"Doesn't matter, does it, old boy?"

"I guess not."

We had lunch in the hotel. I was still bruised and didn't feel like knocking around too much. My nose was sore and there were blue marks around my ribs. I was surprised to find I had ribs left. With every move, my aching muscles made me violently anti-Communist. At lunch we talked about the possibility of Kim-Pak's friends trying to score on us again. Leslie wasn't worried about it; he felt they wouldn't move again until we did.

"And when do we?"

"While you have been splendidly lounging about, old boy, I've been out working. Our end of it is relatively simple. We're to meet Leigh on the border, up by the Sham Chun River. Once we've looked him over to make sure they aren't palming off a phony on us, and once he's had a chat with you, he and the woman simply step across. Our job then will be to get them out of here as quickly as possible. What they have to go through to get to the Sham Chun isn't something we need to know, in fact, you shouldn't know."

"In case the opposition becomes active again, I suppose."

"Yes."

"You're so damned cheerful."

"This round is on me."

After the waiter brought the drinks and moved away, I asked Leslie when the operation would take place.

"Frankly, I'm a little worried about the timing, Michael."

"What do you mean?"

"As set up earlier, it was to have taken place tonight."

"My God! Hadn't we better be out doing something?"

"I've done everything possible. Now we just wait."

"We're not on schedule."

"No."

"What went wrong?"

"I don't know."

"How do you know we're behind schedule, then?"

"Leigh and the woman were to have passed a checkpoint. One of our friends was supposed to pass the word. The word hasn't arrived."

"Where is the checkpoint?"

"Canton."

"What have you done about it?" I asked.

He leaned back and sipped on his gin-tonic. "I've sent the word back down the line to find out what the hell's going on. Right about now we're checking on our man in Canton. I should be getting word anytime."

"How will you get it?"

"I'm not trying to be secretive, Michael. It's just that you have no need to know and it's better for you if you don't."

"All right. Tell me what to do and I'll do it."

"Just stick close to your telephone. Incidentally, please don't tamper with the phone. I've got a debugging device in there and you might damage it. It's rather sensitive."

"Okay. Anything else I should know?"

"Yes. There's a pistol under your pillow. I'd like you to learn how to use it. Don't mean to be melodramatic, but you might need it someday. Makes a hell of a paperweight, if nothing else. Keep it as a favor to me. I'll feel better if you have it. Do you want me to show you how it operates, or do you know anything about handguns?"

"Thanks, I'll manage."

"Good. I hope you never need it, but one never knows."

"Leslie, I promise you, if I ever get back to Hawaii, I'm not getting out of the damned house."

"I don't blame you," he said. "I hear the traffic is dangerous."

Leslie went away and I went up to the room. The pistol was a Luger, a very fine one, well-balanced and simple to operate. I felt I could handle it if I had to.

I was still sore but feeling better and thought about going down to the beach and swimming out to the raft just offshore in the center of the bay, but decided against it. I wasn't really feeling all that good, and Leslie had asked me to stay near the telephone. My eye caught the pile of documents and photos on the table and I wandered to the table to look at them again.

That's when I found the portfolio. It was buried under the other material and I hadn't gone very deeply. There were several sheets of paper in a brown envelope and they turned out to be reproductions of some of Leigh's work. I don't know how Leslie—or his friends—got them, because they obviously hadn't been intended for publication and therefore probably not published in China or anywhere else. I sat down to read them.

The first was a letter to someone in England:

DEAR L.,

As you know I have never suffered from a feeling of inadequacy; now, however, I do. It comes upon me when I try to answer your question.

What a question! "What is China like?"

Like nothing you've ever seen, there in that fog-bound island, and like everything you've seen in your imagination.

There are many Chinas.

The Takla Makan. A desert, as you probably know from your geography lessons, in Central Asia, really in what used to be Turkestan. It lies between the Kunlun Mountains and the Tarim River, and it contains all the secrets of the universe, for when a man goes into the Takla Makan, he is forced to turn into himself for the secrets of survival. And that, my dear, is all the universe can offer us, isn't it? Just a new form of survival?

The Yangtze, the Yellow, the Pearl, the Mekong— changing rivers, with rapids and gigantic rocks with birds overhead, rivers that run the wrong way in places, rivers you can step across in some areas, and can't see across in others, rivers that people live and die on, stepping ashore only rarely. The great rivers of China, winding, winding, long fingers of water across the land, snaking from history to history, out of time and beyond the years.

Rivers and deserts, and a fertile rim of good farming

land, and under the soil minerals in abundance, and above the ground that wonder of wonders, that miracle of persistence: the Chinese.

I have yet to meet a Chinese that did not have a sense of seasons, of time passing and history and ancestry and the ordered movement of the sun, and the cruelty of man, and man's temporary status on the earth. It is why he respects the soil so; it will be here when he is gone, and when his son's sons are gone. It is why all Chinese want to be buried in the eternal soil of China. It is the most permanent thing in his awareness.

It is too big, too much. I cannot answer the question. I am sorry.

More mundane things. Yes, I am well. Medical care is good, dental care is terrible. Food, usually, is good, transportation is terrible. I suppose they balance out. I am happy and working hard. My chief complaint is that I cannot get access to the reference works I need to do any serious writing on my own. Despite this, and the long working hours, and various disasters that are boring when retold, I think China is on the way back to the forefront of history and civilization. Wish us luck. Choy-lin, who is well, sends you her best wishes. She is a delight to me. Good-bye.

MALCOLM

I read the letter twice, then put it down. The next sheet of paper seemed to be part of a letter also, and Leigh had been complaining about the weather:

Some sort of Homeric wind, blowing and wailing and the snow behind it, and behind that a sense of force, of some power up in the mountains, moving the weather in chunks all across China.

It's like that occasionally.

I don't know how to tell you that the essence of life in China lies in such elemental things as wind and dust and mountains. Do you remember when we were children how we'd look at the drawings in books that showed China? Those childlike drawings that had a dragon in every picture, until we came to think of Cathay and dragons in the same instant? You may laugh, but I still think that way, after all these years. The only thing is, I've seen the dragon for myself now, and it's everywhere, it's real.

The dragon's breath is this terrible wind; the pounding of stakes by thousands of coolies on a railway project seemed to me the beating of the dragon's heart; and that terrible eye—the secret police—is everywhere. Strange, isn't it? To think I am one facet of the dragon's eye.

And it's true: the eye of the dragon swings and wherever it turns, there is someone left in pain. In the end that will be the thing that causes me to turn upon myself, or flee.

I got up and got a drink and sat down again and went on to the next bit of paper in the portfolio. Leigh had written down some impressions, really just fragments, but they showed his sure, journalistic eye. He wrote:

... dun-colored hills, not unlike Scotland, and blue smoke rising on a blue evening from mud-wall homes with thatched roofs and a smoke hole for cooking indoors, and no sanitation ... an anachronism: a warlord, or former warlord, riding into the village on a starving horse, a knife in a rusty scabbard and gray in his wispy beard. He has come to beg . . . Fong, the village idiot, is the strongest man in the village and therefore feared. Couple this with his fearful temper and you have a man much respected by the other villagers. For Fong it's just as good as being rich . . . in the cities, now, there is clangor and bedlam, with outdoor furnaces going up and failing and coming down and not enough ore being smelted to make any difference. Sometimes we make ourselves ridiculous in the eyes of the world, but in our own eyes we are valiant, determined, brave. We suffer from collective myopia ... why is *south* the magnet, the historical target? It's always the south, the lazy, indolent, carefree south that must suffer when hard-eyed northerners loom out of the cold ... of all the vague expressions in the Chinese language, the li is the most confusing. A man may live so many li away but you never have any idea because the unit of measurement varies from sector to sector. Villagers, peasants reject such measuring units as kilometers ...

I kept looking through the portfolio. There was the irresistable urge to read other people's diaries and mail, and then I thought I might learn a little more about Leigh, the kind of man he had become. There were several other papers, but they were mostly pieces he'd written for publication in various Communist papers around the world, and didn't tell me much. But then I found another one that showed me Leigh in an unguarded moment. It was a letter to his sweetheart:

CHOY-LIN DEAR,

I'm writing you in English instead of Chinese because I can be more precise and because—if you recall—you wanted the practice of reading.

We are almost finished here in Sinkiang, it has been fascinating but I am ready to return to Peking, and you. Frankly, I'm tired and the winter here has been terrible. I feel like Napoleon venturing into Russia and getting stopped by the winter. Much the same has happened here.

Another thing has happened that I must tell you about. They have lied to me and now they are trying to cover up their lies. I suffer from no illusion, labor under no false hopes, but what they have done here with the new roads and airfields simply cannot support their earlier reasons. And they would not let me into Tibet, which infuriated me. I have protested officially to Wu and perhaps the Hsinhua's influence will prevail and I can enter Tibet before I leave. If this comes about, I will be, probably, a month later getting back to you. But no man would pass up a chance to visit the top of the world.

But back to the airfields: There are seven of them and they are being designed to handle the largest Soviet aircraft. The road net connects them, with alternate routes and supply bunkers that can be locked along the route. It obviously is an offensive base for launching attacks against India if such attacks are ordered.

But what annoys me is the deception and lies. They are not new in China (or anywhere else) and my position now allows me to know and evaluate most of the information I get. Naturally the Hsinhua is represented here but the man seems to be largely ineffectual and I shall send out a replacement when I return to Peking.

It was not necessary for them to lie to me; what must be done must be done, within reason, and I recall Bismarck's statement—or was it Swinburne's rephrasing?—

about not with dreams but with blood and iron, etc., etc. The thing that irritates is refusal to let me into Tibet. I am the second-ranking man in Hsinhua, deputy to Wu himself. But when I press for transportation into Tibet, I am told there is no transportation, or the snows have blocked the roads, or the Khamba tribesmen are raiding again, etc., etc., a thousand and one excuses from a clod of a general whose table manners are terrible and political awareness is nil. Perhaps he can be replaced, also. We'll see about that.

But enough. It is irritating but not eternal. Nothing lasts forever, and perhaps when we are a nation in spirit as well as in fact, we can remove these beastly generals and consign them to something for which they truly are suited— killing flies or supervising the rubbish dumps.

I am grateful for the gloves. It has been a cold winter and a long one, and this is a desolate and wind-whipped part of China. I feel old and lonely and frustrated but all will be bright again when I return to you, and may it be soon.

I trust there is sufficient activity in Peking to keep you interested and happy. I shall be with you soon, my dear.

Good-bye.

MALCOLM.

Not much, I suppose, but they told me a little about Leigh and I had a feeling everything I could learn would be of some use. The last letter puzzled me a little. As deputy director in Hsinhua, Leigh should have been able to fire any general in the field, get any transportation he wanted anywhere. It made me curious about the relationship between the army and Hsinhua. China has always been torn by factionalism. It was possible there was a continuing battle between the military and Hsinhua, cliques in opposition and so on. Maybe that was one of the things Leigh would clear up when we got him out. If we got him out.

His letter to Choy-lin bothered me in another way, too. I felt it revealed a certain naiveté that Leigh should have lost long ago in China. He seemed to be making a fuss about someone's lying to him, and if he had spent more than a decade in China without realizing that lies are part of the game, there was something wrong with him. It just didn't seem possible he could complain like a petulant child because he'd been lied to.

With that thought I began to wonder if the portfolio was a plant. Did it really reflect Leigh's attitudes, or were we being one-upped by some bright boy in Peking? And why? Were we being fooled by Leigh himself? If so, why? Were they leading us into a trap? If so, why?

I couldn't think of any reason why they'd want me. I was no spy, no agent, and they must know that. I felt I was a good correspondent, but there must be at least two hundred correspondents spread from Japan to the other end of the East.

So it must be Leslie they wanted.

But that didn't hold up, either. If they wanted Leslie out of the way, it wouldn't have to be staged in such an elaborate—and therefore fallible—manner. They'd simply send out a team of assassins to get him, and I knew enough about Asia to know if you want a man killed, you can get him eventually, no matter how good he is, if he stays in Asia long enough. If they were serious about killing either one of us, for that matter, it would have been done by now. A few chills accompanied that thought.

So they wanted us alive. It meant only for the duration, only until they found out what we were up to. Swinging full circle now, that meant the portfolio wasn't a plant and Leigh was straight and there weren't any deeper games going on under the surface. I hoped.

It was enough to give a man a headache; I got up to get a little preventive medicine from the liquor stand when the telephone rang. It was Leslie.

"Hello, chum. Things all right?"

"I've been sitting here thinking of all the things that could go wrong," I said. "Working myself into a case of acute melancholia. You got any cures?"

"Have a drink."

"I'm doing that. What's happening?"

There was a pause. I had come to dread it when Leslie paused. "There's a sort of complication, old boy," he said.

"Well, just lay it on me. I'm too old to be sensitive anymore."

"All right. You may start packing. We're going home."

I couldn't believe it. "Home?"

"Righto. Everything's hurtled to a sudden stop and it's all been called off. Mission's over or off, either way you choose to think of it."

"Somehow I can't get too worked up about that," I said.

"Neither can I. Hang around a bit, though, won't you? I'll be over in a couple of hours and help you celebrate."

"All right," I said, and put down the receiver and walked over and mixed a drink and sat down again to think.

It wasn't supposed to end this way. In all the spy stories everything rocketed toward a neatly wrapped ending, happy or unhappy, and nobody went home until the job was done. We were going home without getting the job done.

I began to get restless all of a sudden, experiencing a slight letdown, like a mountain climber all set to try for the top and then told the weather was bad. I set the half-finished drink down and walked out, closing the door, and went down the steps and through the lobby. It was hot and humid outside and the wind had died. I went down to the sand and took off my loafers and socks and walked near the water's edge.

There was a shout above me and I looked up. Leslie was grinning cheerfully and waving. I walked out of the sand and put on my shoes and socks again and hiked back up the wide stone steps to where he was standing beside the road.

" 'Allo, chum," I said, mocking him. "Won't you join me in a ruddy old lemon squash?"

Still smiling, he spoke softly. "Just hang onto that silly grin while we walk out on the terrace."

Despite his warning, the grin almost slipped. I didn't like the edge in his voice and the cloudy look in his eyes. I fell in beside him and we sauntered toward the far table, for all the world like a couple of friends enjoying the Orient and each other's company.

"There's a hell of an empty feeling where my stomach used to be," I said. "And the old buzzer is going in the back of my head. I have a feeling you're going to tell me we're in trouble again."

He turned a cheerful face to me and said quietly, "Things are in a bloody mess. Our agent in Canton is dead. A safe house we had in Macao was raided by the Portuguese cops because they were tipped it was full of heroin. It was. Put there by somebody else. Our people there are in the jug and it's going to be damned touchy getting them out. You might try smiling again, just in case somebody's tagging us. No use giving it all away, you know."

I smiled, I thought.

It brought a genuine grin from Leslie. "You look bilious," he said. We reached the table and sat down. A waiter, irritated at having to walk so far to serve us, came up and crossly took our order. I was beginning to feel like an alcoholic; I really needed a drink.

"All right," I said wearily. "Now what?"

"Mind feeling under your chair first, Michael? And under your side of the table? We used this table once before. If you find any wires, I'll have a look."

I ran my hands under the table and chair. Leslie was doing the same and even examining the ashtray.

"Find anything?" he asked.

"Nothing but old chewing gum," I said disgustedly.

The waiter was back. I signed the chit and he went away again. Leslie, looking rather unhappy now, took a long swallow, crossed his legs and said conversationally, "Sorry I got you into this. I didn't want to originally, you know."

"Don't worry about it, Les. I'm not really sorry. Don't feel bad about it, for Christ's sake. Just tell me what's to be done from here on out."

He took another long drink. I realized this had been a lot rougher on him than on me.

"The fellow in Canton was a friend of mine," he said. "I liked him very much. We keep losing the good ones."

I thought of Kim-Pak's sacrifice. "So do they," I said.

"Yes. Both sides, we lose the professionals because their luck runs out or because we get to know each other so well we form opinions about each other and it affects your work. Well, hell with that. What's to happen now, you asked. Number one, I've got to go to Macao. You can come along if you like, but I'd rather you didn't——"

"So you won't have to worry about me," I interrupted.

"Something like that. Mind sticking around here?"

"I thought we were calling it off. You said——"

"That was for the benefit of the opposition, in case they were listening. Wait till you hear number two."

"I'm waiting."

"We're leaving, all right. When I get back from Macao. Two days at most, then we're pulling out."

"But not going home."

"Righto."

"Where?"

"South."

I said a few profane things and took a long pull of my drink. "South," I repeated. "The monsoon will be here soon."

"I know, I know. We have to go."

"Explain."

"My chum in Canton is dead. Our safe house in Macao is inoperative. Both of us are known by sight now, and undoubtedly being watched. It's too risky to go on with the original idea."

"So Leigh and the woman aren't coming over here."

"No," said Leslie. "Plans are changed. We think they're getting suspicious. They may start watching Leigh and, if so, the moment he gets near the New Territories, they'll throw a guard around him and ease him back into China. No, we can't get him out here."

"Does he know this?"

"He's been told and is changing his plans. So we have to change ours."

"All right," I said. "You get back from Macao and then we go get him, right? Where's it to be?"

"Southeast Asia. I don't know where just yet."

I looked across the table at his handsome face. Despite the shootings and danger and uncertainty—to say nothing of the boredom, discomforts and day-to-day tension—I had a feeling Leslie liked this sort of life. I sure as hell didn't.

"You limey bastard," I said. "You'll get me in trouble yet."

 **six**

THE PLANE WENT IN LOW OVER THE RICE paddies and the carabao and banked left for the approach to Don Muang. When the left wing dipped in the bank I could see the long, glaring ribbon of concrete runway and almost could feel the heat waves bouncing on it, and a minute later we were bouncing from it as the plane touched down and jolted up again before settling and rolling down the concrete.

Even as we rolled, the air inside the plane grew warm. It felt like a movable sauna.

We braked and turned and the engines sighed to a stop. Looking out the window, I saw we were a good seventy-five yards from the terminal and wondered again why they can't drive the damn planes up to the terminal like they do everywhere else in the world.

The door swung open and let in a blast of humid air every bit as debilitating as the air inside the plane. At the same time the stewardess announced that the bus to the terminal had broken down and we would have to walk to the customs area. Fortunately the baggage cart was still operable; I thought that pretty good for this particular airport.

I looked around at Leslie in the seat beside me. He shrugged and unfastened his seat belt and we pushed our way out into the aisle to join the other passengers. We went out and down the ramp, where the stewardess, waiting at the bottom, announced her regret at the inconvenience. Before we had walked the first twenty yards, I felt my shirt starting to stick to my back and my collar felt like a noose.

After the customs area the terminal itself was cool and I was pleased to find the air conditioning on and working. It was a large terminal and hadn't changed since the last time I had seen it. I remembered the dull green rugs and the plastic-covered couches and the feeling of space. Not many Thais flew anywhere in airplanes, so the lobby held only a few tourists, mostly Westerners, taking refuge from the heat beyond the tinted windows.

Leslie had said the enemy camp would be watching the airports for us. I looked around to see if I could spot the opposition. There were the tourists and a bearded, turbaned Indian and some enlisted pilots of the Royal Thai Air Force and a few terminal maintenance men and baggage crews. It looked very peaceful to me.

We walked over to the money exchange and swapped dollars for baht and went out to haggle with a taxi driver. Leslie ruled out the sam lors, the Thai version of a rickshaw, and we squeezed with our luggage into an ancient Datsun.

Ten minutes later, on our way to Bangkok, we bounced off the dirt road onto a paved one, smoother generally but full of spine-jarring holes. Off to the right I could see a building I recognized, a monument to Thai planning. It was a railway station out in the middle of a field. It sat there empty because after the station was built, the firm went bankrupt and couldn't lay the tracks to it. It was a train station without trains or tracks and it was symbolic, somehow, of all the grandiose plans that fail and the brilliant ideas that never quite work out.

On the left was a domed temple topped by a tall stupa and beyond that I could see the glimmer of a klong, a canal, and a few minutes later we were on the iron bridge crossing the klong. Below were the river people on sampans, but most of the sampans were on the dry banks because the klongs, at this time of year, were nearly dry. The coming monsoon would raise the water level as much as ten feet in some places, and the river people would be more mobile and more prosperous, getting their vegetables to market by sampan while the vegetables still were fresh. It was a hell of a hard living. It was all they knew. So many things in Asia were like that: living was tough because that's all the people knew about farming, or so-and-so was a leader because he had a gun, or the mob demonstrated because there were so many of them and it was a hot night, or she became a street-walker because it was an easier life than rice-farming and she had parents to support.

"There's the Temple of Dawn," Leslie said.

I turned my head and saw the Wat Arun towering in the distance, one of Bangkok's landmarks, a complex of Buddhist temples with a high tower from which you could see a good deal of the city. It also got you above the smells from the nearby floating fish market.

We were approaching the war memorial that commemorated a victory over Burma sometime before 1939 when this country was still Siam, before the name was changed to Thailand. It was an ugly memorial to an ugly war, but most streets wound to it sooner or later, and the driver started chattering away in Thai.

"I think he wants to know where we're going," I told Leslie. "He will have to branch off at the memorial. Where do you want to stay?"

"I don't care," he said. "Erawan. Or the Oriental?"

"How about the Palace?" I asked. "It's convenient."

"Fine," Leslie said, and spoke very clearly in English to the driver: "Pat Pong Road. Palace Hotel." The driver nodded and a few minutes later we made a hard right and started past King Phumiphon's palace and down toward Pat Pong. We had skirted several carabao on the way in, but now we were in the city and the traffic was shocking. Cars from all over the world roared challengingly down the streets, weaving and racing, and pedestrians danced among them, apparently accustomed to danger, and made for the opposite side of the street. I spotted a few new buildings under construction, but generally Bangkok was the same blend of modernity and tradition and the street noises were deafening and the smells unbelievable. We rounded the corner where the USIS library still stood—some kind of longevity record for the USIS libraries in Asia—past the United Press International office and across from the Japanese cafe, and stopped in front of the Palace.

I liked the Palace because the food was good and the rooms adequate and air-conditioned and cheaper than the imposing Erawan, where all the visiting notables holed up. In the cool, comfortable lobby of the Palace we got checked in, ordered drinks sent up with us, and crowded into the small elevator that inched its way to our floor. A few minutes later we were isolated from the heat and noise and sipping drinks and shedding clothes. I took a quick bath and sat on the edge of one of the beds, a towel around me, finishing off the drink. Leslie was eyeing me.

"You look a lot better, old man," he said.

It was true. The blue bruise-spots had faded from my chest and ribs and my stomach had lost that mottled, angry redness that came from Kim-Pak's heroes slamming fists into it. My nose was still a little sore, but my breathing was not affected and there would be only a small scar. I hoped I wouldn't run into that sort of thing again.

"Well," I said. "We're here. Now what?"

"Let's check the place out," he answered, and got up and did just that. He did the obvious things first: unscrewing all the light bulbs, looking at the backs of the dresser drawers, crawling under the beds and checking behind the paintings on the wall. Then he went over the room again, making sure the drapes were closed so nobody could aim a listening device in on our conversation from outside, knocking on the walls for the hollow sound that would mean a hidden microphone, plugging his electric razor into all the outlets to make sure they were outlets instead of hidden amplifiers. Then he went out into the hallway and knocked around, checking out the lock, loosening the lock with a small pocketknife to make sure it was merely a lock.

All the while I sat on the bed and watched with a mixture of admiration and amusement.

"You look like a boy scout working on a merit badge," I told him.

"Got their start in England," he grunted. "Don't forget Lord Baden-Powell."

"The old boy wouldn't approve of you, Leslie."

"Only because of the company I keep."

He came back inside and closed the door, then got up again. "Talk in a normal tone, say anything, just keep talking." He walked out and closed the door and I started in on a few lines of poetry. In a moment Leslie was back in the room.

"Can't hear you outside," he said. "We're all right here."

"Good," I said. "Back to the question. Now what?"

"We wait for contact. One of us in the room at all times. We'll be joined by a man who will have the answers. He'll be the end of a string that reaches right into Peking, Michael. And he'll know where Leigh is and how to get him out."

"It didn't work so well in Canton."

"There are many threads in a string, old boy. Leigh and the woman headed that way and our agents got active in preparation for getting them across. The opposition couldn't figure out what was going on but they knew something was, and just as they did with Old Wu, they knocked off our boy in Canton. One of our boys in Canton."

"Did he tell them anything, do you suppose?"

"No," said Leslie. "He had a pill."

I couldn't think of anything to say to that.

"When he was picked up, the news went back up the thread. Leigh and the woman knew about it in time to change their route," Leslie continued. "They've swung south. They can't get out in Vietnam because there's just too damned much activity, so it'll be in one of several other places. Bangkok happens to be the center of things, so we can get from here to there whenever we get the word."

"Have any idea when that will be?"

"Soon, I think. The opposition aren't the only ones with people watching us. Our side knows we're here, by now right down to our room number."

"How do you know we—your friends—aren't making the

same mistake? About getting active? maybe the other side
will react the same way it did in Canton."

"No," he said slowly. "They didn't learn anything from
that. All they got was a dead agent, which doesn't help them
any. They want to know what's in the wind. And I imagine
they're getting a little nervous about not knowing, by this
time."

"Okay, that about does it, I guess. Did you get everything
straightened out in Macao? You were gone only overnight."

"It was quick because I got authorization to use a little
money. You can go a long way out here with the right kind
of funds, you know. Of course our safe house is blown, but
we're setting up another one and my people are out of jail."
He smiled, and added, "There's a shriveled little old man
with a green eyeshade and sleeve garters sitting back in a
musty closet right this moment, having a heart attack because he's comptroller in charge of funds and I have just
damn near bankrupted him."

"Sounds fascinating," I said. "I wish you'd tell me more
about this organization. Are you one of the fair-haired lads?"

"Good God, no, Michael. I'm just one of the field hands. I
wish you could see the whole operation. For that matter I
wish I could see it all. I only know part of it, the part I need
to know. I prefer it that way, and it's one of the house rules
anyway."

"And do you have a pill, too, Leslie?"

"Yes."

"I don't want one," I said. "It would depress me. And I
might take it some drunken morning under the impression it
was an aspirin."

"Don't worry, I hadn't planned on giving you one. I'm
hoping we don't get down to that stage."

"What happens if we do?" I asked, suddenly cold.

"I'll try to shoot you first," he said quietly.

After a while I said bitterly, "Thanks a lot."

And we waited.

It became boring after a while, and we started going out
one at a time, to dinner, to wander around the streets,
taking in Bangkok and the Temple of the Reclining Buddha
and the klongs and pretty Thai girls and the Temple of the
Emerald Buddha, and more klongs. One at a time we
shopped for small items in the square across from the

Erawan and sat in the Ambassador watching classic Thai dances or the brutal Thai boxing, in which the boxers are permitted to kick as well as punch. We took in the shows at The Chateau, separately, and had caviar and vodka up on the fifth floor of the Oriental and frogs' legs in wine sauce at the Keynote.

And all the time our thoughts were on Leigh. Where was he now? Was he all right? Was the woman with him? He must be running scared. He would know about the death of the agent in Canton, and it would frighten him. He would know that the operation was not going according to plan. Would he lose faith, turn around, and make it back to Peking and take his chances? I wished I knew more about his situation within the Hsinhua. I wished I knew more about the woman. I asked Leslie about her, but he didn't know much more and none of it important. She was just a name and a face and another facet of trying to get Leigh out of China.

After four days my nerves were getting raw and I started snapping at Leslie whenever we were in the room together. He took it with an easy tolerance and every time I growled, I was immediately sorry and felt like an idiot. But I could feel the tension growing in me and I was impatient to get things moving. Bangkok was a great city, interesting and vibrant and colorful. It was probably the most Oriental-appearing city in the Orient and I'd always liked it and found it charming. Now, however, with the tension and because I could neither go out on the town with Leslie or look up a few acquaintances, I found myself strolling the streets in boredom, wishing I could share this city with someone. Then, back inside the room, I felt cramped and shut in while Leslie was out and irritable and tense while he was there.

"When, Leslie, how soon?"

"I don't know," he would answer, truthfully and patiently.

"I know, I know," I would mutter. "Sorry, Les."

"Don't worry about it, old boy. Can't be helped."

It was a little like the war, a hell of a lot of weariness and boredom shot through with hours or days of stark terror. At least in the war you knew where to find the enemy, if you had to go after him. You knew what he looked like, what you were up against. Leslie, I learned, could sleep anywhere, anytime, and for as long as he wanted. He slept a good bit of the time, finding refuge in it. I couldn't. I read a lot, and drank a lot, and swore a little more readily than usual, covering everything that irritated me at the moment, from the Hsinhua to the harmless lizards insect-hunting on the windows.

Then our contact turned up.

It was the morning of the ninth day after we had arrived in Bangkok. As it happened, both Leslie and I were in the room. There was a soft knock and I walked over to open it. Leslie stepped behind the door and thumbed the safety off the gun he was holding.

Standing in the hallway was a mild, middle-aged man in a rumpled pair of trousers and a graying white shirt, with the belt too big for the pants and his black shoes scuffed and dirty. He could have been one of a million or so Thais you passed on the street and never noticed.

Until he spoke, that is. He had a voice that sounded as if it were coming from the bottom of a well. It was deep and powerful and, coming from that frail body, incongruous. Before I could speak, he looked up at me and said in quite clear and only faintly accented English, "Ah, how do you do. I am looking for two friends. You are one of them," and he smiled.

I hesitated, then swung open the door, because out of the corner of my eye I could see Leslie put the safety back on and replace the gun in his shoulder holster. He was starting to grin.

"Let him in, Michael," he said. "It's Uthanipan. Buddha's gift to Radio Bangkok."

"Hello, Mr. Trent," the small man said, stepping inside and reaching for Leslie's hand. They greeted each other like old friends, which, as it turned out, they were.

We sat on the beds, Uthanipan and I sizing each other up. I offered to ring for room service and order drinks.

"He doesn't drink," said Leslie. "Doesn't smoke. Doesn't swear or gamble or chase women." He turned and smiled affectionately at Uthanipan. "His only vice is patriotism. Right?"

The small Thai nodded. "Mr. Trent is right. I love my country. We have never been a colony of another power. We are the only nation in Southeast Asia that has never been colonized. The Communists want to rule us. I will not allow it."

He made the last statement with assurance. I started to like him.

"Uthanipan is an announcer, as you've probably guessed by that voice. Radio Bangkok. Does a lot of work for Radio Free China as well, and when he isn't being a patriot or making love to that lovely wife of his, he works for the organization."

"And," said Uthanipan, "that is why I am here."

Finally, I thought. Finally and at last.

"Can we talk here?" he asked. Leslie nodded.

Uthanipan's voice rounded off each syllable, but he didn't waste any words when he got right down to business. "Check out early tomorrow and take a taxi to Don Muang. Buy two tickets for Rangoon. There's a flight at ten o'clock, and I've already made reservations in your name. After you buy the tickets, go into the bar and talk about the flight and about the bargains in Rangoon. Let them load your luggage; I'm afraid you'll have to write that off in expenses. Before boarding time, just before, wander out onto the apron on the west end of the terminal building. Try not to be followed. Once you get outside, you'll have to hurry. There will be a helicopter waiting. A black one, unmarked, and it will be warming up. There will be a pilot and copilot, both Americans. One of them will ask you a question. No matter what he asks, you are to answer with the name of our queen, Sirikit. Is it clear to you, thus far?"

"Yes," I said. "Does that helicopter belong to Air America?"

"Yes," he answered. "It does."

I knew Air America. Its pilots and crewmen were paid by the Central Intelligence Agency and were damned good.

"Please continue," said Leslie.

"The helicopter will fly you up-country. It will land once to refuel. You will stay inside. You must not be seen. The second time the helicopter lands, you will be in Laos."

I thought that one over.

"Where in Laos?" Leslie asked.

"At a point halfway between the Mekong River and the city of Vientiane," Uthanipan said. "There will be a car waiting to drive you into Vientiane. You will go into town, meet our clients at the Constellation Hotel, and escort them back by the same car to where the helicopter will be waiting. The four of you will be flown back the same way to Don Muang, met by another car from the American embassy in Bangkok. It will drive you across the field to a waiting airplane, which will fly you into Manila. You will be under diplomatic immunity. At Clark Air Force Base near Manila you will be placed on a special jet aircraft and flown to the United States. You will be met there, and that is the extent of my knowledge. But not, of course, of my concern for your safety."

"Why don't you just send the chopper up and get them?" I asked.

"Because, Mr. Hawkins, Leigh has said he wants to chat with you before making up his mind."

I had a sudden thought: "What if he changes his mind?"

"We'll kidnap him," said Leslie simply.

I mulled that over and didn't like it much, but there didn't seem to be much I could do about it, either.

"What if there's trouble?" Leslie asked. "Can we count on help from the Thais? I wouldn't think so, though."

"No," said Uthanipan. "My government must not become involved. We must do all we can to preserve our neutrality, although it is obvious where our sympathies lie and where we get our aid."

I didn't know much about operations like this. I asked if the plan were complicated or simple, in relation to other, similar operations. Leslie assured me it was a simple plan, therefore a good one.

Uthanipan chatted for a few minutes with Leslie, then rose and we shook hands all around and he left. It had taken only thirty minutes for him to arrive, brief us, wish us luck and leave. I hoped the rest of the operation would be as simple.

It was a large, black UH-type helicopter, spotted right where Uthanipan had said it would be. There was no point in trying to hide it, so the pilot didn't. I suppose the idea was just to get the damned thing in the air and let it disappear from those watching us on the ground. And we all knew somebody was watching us; it would be too much to hope for that we weren't being watched.

I looked at the far end of the runway. The plane was warming up for the flight to Rangoon. Passengers were streaming toward it and it was going to be very clear very soon that we weren't among them. I looked at Leslie. He was searching the airport with his eyes. Then he turned and nodded and we started loping out to the helicopter.

The rotor blades were turning and I went in low from the

side and straight to the open door. There was no flight crewman, so I just piled in, dropped into a canvas seat, and started hooking up the belt. Leslie was doing the same.

Down through the shaft that separates the crew from the passengers I could see the feet of the two men who were to fly us to Laos. Then one of them leaned down and motioned for us to put on the two headsets so we could talk via intercom. When Leslie and I had adjusted them, the copilot asked for a password. We were silent. The next voice was that of the pilot. It came across the intercom in a hard, nasal, Texas twang, and he asked us when the monsoon was due. He made monsoon sound like three or four words. I looked over at Leslie and he nodded and I said quietly, "Sirikit."

The copilot leaned down again and motioned to Leslie to shut the sliding door. A few seconds later we were rolling a bit down the runway and then the airport dropped away and the air was much cooler and we were flying smoothly with no turbulence.

The copilot's voice crackled in my ears. "Morning, gentlemen. We'll be heading off on about two hundred twenty degrees in a minute, just to confuse our friends on the ground. We'll be swinging back northeast after that, so just relax. We'll stop at a refueling point north of Song Hong. Please stay in the aircraft."

"Okay," I said. "Always good to fly with an experienced airline."

The next voice in the earphones belonged to the pilot again. He seemed annoyed as hell about something: "You do yore job and we'll do ours, okay?"

"Sorry," I said. "Just trying to make a small joke."

We flew in silence for a while. I looked around the helicopter. There wasn't a marking inside it that would have identified it as coming from any particular country.

The pilot's voice twanged at us again. "Didn't mean to sound like a horse's ass a minute ago," he said. "Uthanipan was a friend of mine. Guess it still bothers me a little."

Leslie and I looked at each other, startled. "Sorry, chum, we don't follow you," I said.

"I said Uthanipan was an old friend. Knowed him ever since I been out here," the pilot said.

"We heard that," said Leslie. "But what does it mean?"

"You mean you ain't heard?" The pilot's voice held a note of surprise.

"No," Leslie almost whispered, but by that time we knew what was coming.

"They found him this mornin'," said the pilot. "In a klong off the Chao Phraya."

"Dead," I said.

"Yeah," the pilot said. "Shot twice, once in the chest and once in the back of the head. Looked like somebody suckered him out there and shot him and when he didn't die fast enough, they gave him the old Asian send-off. They must have shot him with a Magnum. Wasn't very pretty."

I looked over at Leslie. His head was bowed and he looked tired and sad. After a while he asked, "What about his wife and children?"

"We'll take care of 'em," the pilot said. "We always do."

"I'd like to help," Leslie said.

"Quit blamin' yoreself," the pilot said. "Ain't yore fault. Best thang you can do is do yore job. He got killed so you could, I guess. Be an awful shame if it didn't work out now. Kinda like he got killed for nothin'."

"We'll do the job," said Leslie. "You just get us there."

I sat back and closed my eyes. There was a little turbulence now and the helicopter was jolting a little and I was getting chilled in my thin summer clothes.

Finally the sudden lift of my stomach told me the pilot was easing the helicopter down. Then we started dropping fast and the air turned warmer. I looked out one of the small round windows. All I could see were rice paddies and an occasional stand of trees and a few huts off in the distance. We were dropping very fast and the ground moved up and in a minute all I could see was dust outside from the wind kicked up by the rotors. The engine whined to a stop and Leslie and I sat quietly while the chopper was refueled. I didn't even bother to look outside again.

It didn't take very long; we were airborne again about the time my shirt had been soaked through with sweat and my jacket was starting to get damp. This time we went straight up, no rolling, just straight up and into a steep bank and then off on a straight, gradually climbing course. I leaned back and closed my eyes again.

When I opened them, we were over Laos.

"Either one of you gentlemen ever been in Laos before?" the copilot asked.

"Both of us," I answered.

"Okay," he said. "Here's the drill. We can't go into the strip because the customs types sell information to anybody with enough kip. And speaking of kip, remind me to give you a bankroll soon as we sit down, will you? We'll land just over the Mekong on a side road that leads into the paved road into Vientiane. You know the one I mean. There's a driver there with a car. He'll haul you straight into town. We'll gas up again and wait, however long it takes. The driver will hang around the Constellation until you're ready to pull out. Get out as quickly as you can and get back to us. We'll set you all down at Don Muang."

"Why the Constellation?" I asked. "It's the middle of town."

"I don't know," said the voice in my earphones. "It's just the way it was set up, I guess."

I heard Leslie asking curiously, "Do you know who's coming back with us?"

This time it was the pilot who answered.

"Nope. Don't want to know. Just you two and two others. That's all I wanta know about it, too. Don't tell me no more."

"Can't say as I blame you, old boy."

I looked out the porthole again. We were over a river, following its curve in the direction of the flow. That would be the Mekong and we apparently had swung north and were heading in fast downriver for a quick landing on the Laos side. As we started down, fast, I spotted a good-sized town on the Thailand side. Nong Khai. By Thai standards a nice little town.

As we came down out of the sun I could feel the dusk creeping up. It would be dark in a moment, which was fine with me. Twilights are very short in Southeast Asia. The sun drops like a ball of fire and the nights are waiting and come on fast after the sun is gone.

The wheels touched and the copilot cracked. "Welcome to Laos," and the helicopter shuddered to a stop. It had been a long flight and I felt it as I unbuckled the seat belt and stood and stretched. The sliding door slammed open with a bang and a small Lao in a red beret and carrying a Sten gun motioned us out. We clambered stiff-legged down from the helicopter as the flyers came around the front, the copilot holding out a bundle of money with one hand and waving us into a huddle with the other. He seemed very young for this type of work.

The pilot came up and jerked a thumb at the small Lao. "Yore driver," he said. "Name's Sinn. From what I hear of him they named him right. But you can trust him."

"How long can you wait?" Leslie asked the pilot.

"Till you git back," he said. For the first time we shook hands all around and Leslie and I fell in behind Sinn and followed him to the car. The two helicopter pilots already were turning their attention to their aircraft.

The car was a Citroen that must have been old when Napoleon was emperor, but it started with the first flick of the driver's wrist and we roared away from the helicopter, bounced a couple of times, and were off down the rutted dirt road.

The ground was hard and dry and there was dust everywhere. I glanced behind us and could see the cloud we were leaving, hanging there in the still, humid dark. In front of us the headlights showed a narrow road with the jungle pressing in close and thousands of insects in the beam of our light, some of them splattering against the windshield.

Sinn had taken off his beret and stuffed it into his shirt. The Sten was under the front seat, where it couldn't be seen but where he could reach it quickly. Leslie sat in the front, not talking. I think he was still thinking of Uthanipan, and of Old Wu and the man in Canton and wondering where it was going to end, measuring the deaths against Leigh's life, Leigh's information. We both felt it then, I think, because we were getting close. If all went well, we would meet Leigh and the woman in about an hour. Give me another hour to talk with him, another hour to get back, and we'd have him safely in the chopper and on the way south. If all went well, we could have him in Manila tomorrow. If all went well, I could be home in Hawaii in two or three days.

We slammed off the dirt road and onto pavement and Sinn pressed the accelerator. It was a fairly good road, for Asia, with only the minimum number of holes that never got filled up and spilled gravel that never got cleared away, which could cause your car to slide completely off the road before you knew what was happening. Sinn, whatever else, was a swift and accomplished driver and I began to have confidence in him.

A few miles from where we had turned onto the paved road, he stopped the car. We got out and looked and listened, but there didn't seem to be any other cars around. The few taxis in Vientiane seldom ventured this far out of town. We slapped at the mosquitoes and wiped our faces with handkerchiefs and finally got back in and headed once more toward the city.

Now that we were getting closer to the end, I started thinking about what I would say to Leigh. I didn't have any sort of speech in mind. The best thing was simply to answer his questions as honestly as I knew how to do and assure him he'd be safe in America. I wondered if he'd heard how we had treated the turncoats from the Korean War who had drifted back to the United States. I assumed he had. I remembered a Soviet agent who had gotten asylum in the U.S. and dropped into anonymity. No reason why it wouldn't work for Leigh. Even with the woman along.

The woman puzzled me, too. How did they meet? When did they come to trust each other? How did she manage to tell the deputy director of Hsinhua that she was anti-Communist? And how did he reconcile that with his ideological beliefs, his position of importance, his sense of China's destiny?

He must love her; they must be in love.

Was that enough for a man like Leigh? Was there more?

The car swerved to miss a water buffalo being led by a child, walking in the darkness alongside the road. There were a few lights now, in the huts silhouetted here and there. We were getting into the outskirts of town. Looming up and then dropping past in the darkness was the half-completed war memorial on the south side of the city. It had been half-completed when I saw it last, a couple of years before. Laos was like that: too poor or too civilized to complete a memorial to a war. I didn't know which.

We started to pass a few cars, taxis carrying government officials off to meetings or trysts or wherever government officials went after dark in Vientiane. There were more houses and an occasional office building and then we were on a cobblestone street, wide but bumpy, and getting close. I could feel the anticipation growing in me as we swung around the corner leading to the main street. Then we were on the street and rolling smoothly toward the Hotel Constellation, on the right halfway down the street. A few moments later Sinn stopped the Citroen in front of the hotel and Leslie and I climbed out. There was a long moment while we looked at each other. I thought I saw a slow smile starting at the corners of Leslie's mouth.

Then, without a word, we turned and headed into the Constellation for our meeting with Malcolm Leigh.

seven

WE SAW HER AT THE SAME TIME. SHE WAS sitting at a low table off to the right of the entrance in the lobby that doubled as a bar. There was tea in a cup in front of her on the table, but it looked as if she hadn't touched it. She was alone.

I glanced quickly around the lobby. There were a few Air America crews drinking beer and eyeing two French-Lao beauties at a nearby table, and at another table a man I vaguely recognized, a *Paris-Match* correspondent. He waved a greeting and looked like he might want to chat, but I waved back and turned quickly and Leslie and I moved among the tables over to the woman.

She spotted us, but I couldn't read the expression on her face; it was gone quickly and then she was composed and calm and she watched us approach.

My own expression must have been one of admiration. She was even more beautiful than the photo I had seen and the body encased in a shimmering Thai silk sheath was a match for her face. Her skin was flawless and her eyes had that great, liquid quality that would drive a man to any extreme to keep the tears from them.

She reached out a hand as we came up to the table. Her grip was firm and cool and her voice was steady.

"How do you do, gentlemen?" she said in English. "I am Chang Choy-lin."

We sat. There was a moment when we studied each other in silence; then Leslie asked in a low voice, "Where is he?"

"Upstairs," she said. "We have been waiting for you."

"What's important now is how soon we can move again," said Leslie. "He'll want to talk with Michael, I assume. Immediately he does, we should be moving along. Can you fetch him down, or perhaps we should go upstairs?"

She hesitated. "It is Mr. Hawkins he wanted to see. Perhaps I should take him up while you wait here, Mr. Trent."

Leslie nodded and I rose. She got up and moved toward the stairs and I could feel the eyes of the other people in the lobby following her sinuous walk as she headed for the stairs. I couldn't blame them.

We went up two flights of very narrow steps and down a long, carpeted hallway. I glanced behind me frequently and as the woman turned toward a doorway I pulled out the Luger and flicked off the safety. Too many people had gotten killed around me lately and I had made up my mind to be damned cautious.

Just before she unlocked the door, she looked at the gun in my hand. "You won't need that," she said.

"You'd be surprised what's been happening the last few days," I answered. She didn't reply. She just turned the key in the door and swung it open and stepped into the room in front of me.

I went in quickly, moving to one side with my back against the wall. At first I didn't see him. The room was dark except for a dim table lamp. It was a comfortable but not opulent room and furnished out with plenty of chairs.

Leigh wasn't in any of them. He sat on the floor in a corner of the room, his knees drawn up and his arms locked around them. He was peering at me through a shock of graying hair that had fallen down in front of his face.

And then he spoke. "I want my nanny," he said.

I was stunned.

"I want my nanny," he said again peevishly.

I swung around to Chang Choy-lin.

She closed the door quietly and nodded her head. "Yes," she said. "He's insane."

My mouth was dry and my mind a blank and I stood there for a while with the Luger still in my hand, the woman watching me quietly and Leigh, after speaking twice, ignoring me and putting his face in his arms.

Finally I pushed the safety back on the gun and stuck it back in the waistband of my pants. I could feel my stomach knotting. I looked at Choy-lin.

"Three men have died to get a crazy man out of China," I whispered, hearing the hoarseness in my voice. "You can raise that if you count the other side. Pretty funny, isn't it?"

She didn't answer.

"How long has he been this way?"

"Not long," she said quietly. "A few days. It's been terrible." And with that she put her face in her hands and I could see her shoulders jerking as she cried silently. She must have been through a hell of a lot.

"Go downstairs and get Leslie," I said.

"No," she replied. "Not yet. Please try to talk with him. He's mentioned your name over and over. Perhaps you can help him."

I looked at Leigh, still huddled in the dim corner. "All right," I said, and walked over and squatted near him.

"Leigh? Remember me? I'm Michael Hawkins."

His head came up and he looked at me coldly. "Of course I remember you," he said. "Don't be an ass. Did you bring my nanny along with you?"

"Leigh, she couldn't make the trip. It's a long, hard trip But I can take you to her. I can take you to safety and comfort. You'd like that, wouldn't you?"

He didn't answer.

"Leigh," I pressed on, "if you'll go with us, help us make a little journey, everything will be all right. Will you do that?"

He looked up again. "Why didn't you bring her?" he asked.

I stood up and turned to the woman. "Go down and get Leslie," I said. "Now."

Without a word she turned and went out. I moved over and sat on the edge of one of the two beds and put my chin on my hands and tried to think. I almost didn't hear Leigh's soft call.

"Hawkins?"

"Yes?"

"Listen to me," he said, with an urgency in his voice. "If we can get out, will I be all right? I trust you. You're the only one I know now in the West. Can we make it? Will they treat me decently? You must tell me, and quickly."

"Of course, Leigh. You'll be all right. The only problem

you'll face is just getting out. We've lost three men already and we've been watched into Bangkok. But you'll be all right if we get you out. You've got to trust us."

But then the evenness of his voice dropped into a querulous, old man's tone and he grumbled, "You should have brought my nanny." Just as he said it Leslie and Choy-lin hurried into the room.

"Michael——" Leslie began.

"Yeah, Leslie. It's true. He's crazy."

Leslie stared at Leigh. After one incurious look back at him, Leigh hid his face again and was silent. Choy-lin stood by, composed now, and I sat on the bed and let the irony of it roll over me without even trying to stop it.

Finally I said, "Apparently it comes and goes, a few moments of rational thought and action and then he withdraws again and wants his nanny, for Christ's sake."

Choy-lin nodded. "That's right. But there are very, very few rational moments."

"All right, God damn it," said Leslie. "We've come this far. We're going to take him out of here. Maybe in the few lucid moments he does have he can help us." He asked the woman, "Will he go or do we have to take him?"

She looked at me and I answered. "He'll go."

"All right, then, let's move it," said Leslie.

Half an hour later we left the room and started down the hallway, Leigh walking along quietly, amiably, with a slight smile on his face. Choy-lin had changed into green slacks and a blouse and carried a jacket. Leslie ordered them to leave everything else.

We caused a slight stir in the lobby, but there was no other way out of the Constellation. We could hear the hum of conversation fade as we rounded the tables and went right out the front door. I thought Choy-lin responsible; no one ever looked better in slacks.

The Citroen pulled up as we stepped out into the night. Sinn, from the inside, threw open both doors and we hurried in, Leslie and Leigh sitting with me in the back and Choy-lin in front. Without a word and with barely a glance at us, Sinn gunned the engine, U-turned in the street, and headed out of the city.

For no reason my warning buzzer started up again. I put it down to nerves and tension, but it worried me all the same. It wasn't wrong very often.

We raced past the cluster of buildings in the center of town, past the English-language bookstore, past the big pagoda complex, and headed west and south on the same road that had brought us in. The huts of the Lao farmers were dark against a sky nearly as dark and there were fewer lights burning. We passed a few people on bicycles and the inevitable carabao plodding along, and twice government jeeps came by in the opposite direction.

I glanced around at Leigh. He had aged some, but gracefully. His hair was graying and there were a few wrinkles, but he was still a handsome man and he wore, in spite of his madness, the air of an intellectual. His clothes were obviously made in China and not of the best quality, but they fit well and he managed to look rather debonair in the middle of a most dangerous period in his life.

We had ridden in silence to the point where the dirt road branched off. Sinn swung the Citroen off onto the dirt road, slowing and trying to miss some of the deep wheel ruts made by ox carts.

Leslie broke the silence. "Pull off," he told Sinn. "Let's stretch our legs and have a little chat."

When the car stopped and Sinn turned off the lights, we got out of the car, looking and listening for a few moments, then Leslie called us around to the side of the car opposite the road. He asked Sinn to take a post across the road, and the little Lao driver hauled out the Sten gun and ambled across the road and disappeared in the bushes. When he was out of earshot, Leslie turned to us. We couldn't see each other's faces in the darkness, just silhouettes. He spoke low and quietly.

"I sent Sinn away because I didn't want him to hear our change in plans. Not that I don't trust him, but because he won't be able to tell anyone else if the opposition tries to persuade him. And they may try. Because I have a nagging feeling they know where we are."

The buzzer in my head sounded like a buzz saw. I was sure he was right. Leigh and Choy-lin were silent.

"Let me make a brief summation here," Leslie continued. "Our negotiations with Leigh started more than a year ago. That's a long time to keep secrets. When my department got involved they were well along and it became our job to do the field work, to actually get Leigh out of China. We've lost three agents in doing so. Why? Because the enemy camp knew we were active, knew it was big, and tried to find out. We know they were on to us right into Bangkok. Someone's had us tagged. Someone has an idea of what we're trying to do, at this point.

"So it figures that to succeed we've got to confuse them now. And the only way to do that is to depart from what they expect us to do."

He spoke directly to Choy-lin. "Now. I need some information from you. When did Leigh become ill? When did you know that he would defect? And what happened in Canton, and how did you get here?"

She reached up and pushed her hair back and tilted her face up at Leslie. "I didn't know Malcolm was leaving China until we had actually started, although we had talked about it. Malcolm was growing sick of bureaucracy and lies and suspicion. Everybody in Hsinhua was jealous of him. One day he started a tour, a series of meetings. I went with him because he urged me to. I didn't know in the beginning that we would be trying to get out. When I found out, I didn't think we could make it; he is watched everywhere. Hsinhua. They keep a watch on all top officials.

"When we got down in Fukien, Malcolm departed from the schedule and we went by train to Canton. He left me in a hotel and went out one night and when he came back, he was disturbed. He told me a man had been killed, that he was to have gotten us to Hong Kong. It made him distrust everyone and he began to wonder if he could even trust Mr. Hawkins, whom he had liked and respected from the days in Korea."

She paused and I glanced at Leigh. He stood with his head cocked, listening.

"Malcolm felt we were being watched, although now I am not so sure. But he felt that we would have to abandon the plans to go to Hong Kong. We were both very frightened at that point," Choy-lin continued. "Then Malcolm decided we would try to get out in the south. We were going to try to fly to Phnom Penh, but that didn't work out, so we thought about trying to get to Burma, on the pretext that Malcolm wanted to meet with some Hsinhua people there."

"And that's when our second man in Canton reached you," Leslie said.

"Yes. He told us we'd have to try to get out through Laos. Actually it wasn't as difficult as we had thought. Malcolm simply told Hsinhua we were going to Kunming to meet with the Hsinhua man there, and we did. Then we flew to Mengtzu and on to Ssumao, then across the border of Laos to an airstrip controlled by the Pathet Lao. They were impressed that a man as important as Malcolm would visit them and they did not argue when we left hurriedly and managed to get through to Luang Prabang and then we came unchallenged to Vientiane."

"How did you explain away his illness, all this time?"

Choy-lin slumped back against the car and ran her hand over her face. "It was terrible," she whispered. "He showed the first signs in Canton, the night your man there was killed. Between Mengtzu and Ssumao he had a terrible breakdown, but I was able to calm him. Fortunately, after that, his rational periods seemed to come at the right times, although some people became suspicious. Once I told them he was drunk. Another time, in Luang Prabang, I told the authorities he was very ill. It actually helped us, that time, because everyone was helpful and no one wanted to disturb us very much."

Suddenly Leigh leaned forward and said, in a loud voice, "It's dark here. Why doesn't someone turn on the lights? I'm afraid of the dark?"

"It's all right, Malcolm," the woman said, moving to his side. She stood close to him and held his hand and he stood looking back at her and didn't speak again.

"All right," Leslie said. "That brings us up to now. How did you know to come to Vientiane?"

Choy-lin turned back to him and answered: "We were met in Luang Prabang by one of your men, a small man with a deep voice. I remember the voice because he could not speak Chinese and we cannot speak Lao, so we talked in English. It was a very large voice for such a small man. He gave us money and told us to wait for you in the Constellation. I got the impression that your second man in Canton had gotten a message through to him. We had to trust him. He seemed to know all about us. He told us where to wait for you and we did. Which answers all of your questions, I believe."

"Yes," said Leslie, and after a short pause he addressed all of us: "The enemy has sought information ever since this operation began. He's killed to get it. Each time he's killed, we've known that he didn't get what he wanted or you two would never have gotten this far. Except for the last time.

The last time he killed, it was your small man with the big voice. His name was Uthanipan and he was a good chum of mine. He was a good man. But at this point we don't know if he talked to them before he died. I would doubt it, but we don't know."

The thought hit me. "That means we're really in the soup," I said.

Leslie nodded. "Right. If he talked before he died, they know what's happening. They will have watched us right through to Vientiane, even to our leaving the Constellation."

Nobody spoke for a moment.

"And that, chums," said Leslie, "would mean that our opposite numbers are somewhere over by the helicopter just waiting to bag us."

And at that moment I heard Sinn's running feet cross the road and his anxious whisper, "Car coming, very fast."

Leslie was the first to move. He started pushing us toward the bushes, talking quickly at the same time. "Get into the brush and stay quiet. I'll join you in a moment. Sinn, you'll give them a chase. Turn the car around, turn the lights on, and let them chase you into Vientiane. Give them a burst from the Sten occasionally. It might keep them nervous and our friends by the helicopter may hear it."

He ran around and rummaged in the glove compartment of the Citroen and was back in a moment. Sinn had the motor started by the time Leslie had slammed the door and seconds later the car's lights stabbed into the night, lighting up the road, the bushes, and the insects.

I grabbed Choy-lin's hand and she reached out the other to Leigh. With me leading, we hastened deeper into the bushes and down a small bank. I could tell by the odor that we were on an embankment leading down to a rice paddy. Halfway down the bank we stopped and stretched out in the grass, Choy-lin silent, Leigh mumbling so low I couldn't catch what he was saying, and me praying there weren't any snakes. I heard Leslie's soft footfalls going away; he had moved to the left of us and nearer the road. He was hoping to get a look at our enemy.

The Citroen had pulled out onto the road. I could hear Sinn impatiently racing the motor, anxious for action. He hadn't long to wait. The noise of the second car came hurrying toward us and then I saw its lights sweep overhead as the car rounded a curve and sped on toward us.

Sinn fired once, a short burst, and the Citroen hurtled away. There were two snap shots from the second car, very close together, and the chase was on. In a matter of seconds both cars were out of sight, but the dust clouds hung over the road for several minutes.

Leslie appeared out of the darkness. "Couldn't see them," he said. "Looked like there might have been several of them in the car. We'd better start moving out of here."

"Are we going to try the helicopter?" I asked.

"No," he said. "Too risky. If they know about it, it's inoperative. They'll have stationed someone there in any case. The boys in the car were simply taking a reccy to see if they could spot us. Sinn's shooting put them off a bit. What we have to do now is get out of here, because when they see only Sinn get out of that car, they'll tear back here and start hunting."

"Okay, where'll it be?" I asked.

"We can't go back into Vientiane," Choy-lin said.

"No," replied Leslie. "We're not far from the Mekong. If we start now, we can hike to the Mekong before dawn and get a boat. Do you know what the river's like south of here, Michael?"

"No. It's wide and sluggish north of here and I think for a few miles south, but I don't know much about it after that. In any case, we'd run the risk of Pathet Lao patrols, wouldn't we? And if we got by them, we'd be in Cambodia, staying on the river. Hell, the Cambodians just might send us back."

"All right," said Leslie. "Let's take a quick look at the alternatives. We can't go back to Vientiane. We might be able to hook up with some friendlies deeper into Laos, but there's no point going back that way. We can't go to Cambodia and we'd surely get bagged somewhere trying to make it to Vietnam. What's left is the most obvious course and one we'll have to take. The problem is, it's the same route that the opposition will take, knowing it's our only way out. That is, back through Thailand, the way it was arranged. What do you say, Michael?"

"I'd say you were right."

"Then, here's what we'll do. We'll hike to the Mekong and get a boat and get over to the Thai side of the river. Then we'll try to get south. They may think we're trying to outrun them down the main roads. But we'll be flanking them and trying to stay inconspicuous and maybe they'll outrun us."

"In any case, the payoff will come in Bangkok," I said. "They'll be looking for us there. If Uthanipan talked—and it appears he did—they'll know about the embassy car and the waiting airplane. Won't they be waiting, too?"

"Only if they can't get us here," Leslie said. "They would prefer grabbing Leigh here in the jungles. The Thai police may take a dim view of this sort of thing happening right there at Don Muang. No, the opposition runs the risk of getting caught by the Thai gendarmes if they play it that way. They'll try it only in desperation and when they get desperate, they make mistakes, like everyone else."

"I'm glad to hear that," I said. "I was starting to get the feeling they were all geniuses, and ten feet tall."

"I'll take the first lead," Leslie said, standing. "Keep close together and in a single line behind me. You last, Michael. We'll swap off occasionally. If you hear any strange noises, let me know. Stay close now."

We got up and moved down the bank. Leslie found the usual path between paddies and we crossed some sixty or seventy yards of rice paddies and came up against heavy brush. He poked around and led us through several yards of very thick underbrush; then we were out in fairly open country, still dry from weeks without rain. We crossed that without incident, topped a little rise, and walked out onto level, open ground. Then it was simply moving along in the dark as quickly as possible, with the Mekong somewhere ahead and the enemy somewhere behind.

Twice in two hours Leslie and I swapped places. Choy-lin hadn't spoken since we started walking. Leigh mumbled occasionally and once he said something very loud in Mandarin, but we ignored it and kept moving and he fell silent again.

After Choy-lin had stumbled twice within a few minutes, we sat down to rest. It was much cooler now, but the exertion of walking sent the sweat down my face and chest. Both Leslie and I were in summer suits and street shoes; they weren't made for walking. We had taken off our ties and stuffed them in pockets. The Luger was rubbing a raw spot on my abdomen as I walked, so I took it out of my pants and dropped it in a pocket of the coat. It was a heavy gun loaded, and I felt a little lopsided as we got up and pushed off.

We were still in single file, Leslie leading, when we ran into heavy brush again. It was so thick we had to slip sideways through it in places. We couldn't risk waiting until morning to look for a path, so we just blundered and threshed and swore and inched on through. I had scratches all over me, as did the others, and my clothes were soaked with sweat. When the night breeze picked up a little, it became chill. It was wonderful country for getting a fever or snakebite or malaria. Or getting nibbled on by a tiger or stepped on by an elephant.

Or eliminated by a determined enemy Intelligence apparat.

Eventually we realized no one was behind us. They would be either trying to figure out our direction, or making plans to cut us off somewhere ahead. They had no chance of tracking us through what we'd just come through. We eased up on the pace and about the same time the terrain became gentler and we were able to walk at something near a normal pace. A couple of hours later we walked down and stood on a slope of the turbid, twisting Mekong River.

It was too dark to see across it, but I knew Nong Khai was on the other side. If we could reach it, we'd be in Thailand. Then we would have to think about a route south.

"This way," Leslie whispered, and we walked, a little weary now, after him. There was only a little brush on the bank and he wasn't difficult to follow. Dimly I saw what he was heading for—a crude wooden pier and, tied to it, several sampans.

We huddled. "Can't risk being seen," Leslie said. "Have to steal one. Can't get one with a motor. Too much noise. I'll nip off down there and be back in a moment. I hope you feel like rowing. Just pretend we're punting on the Thames."

"You bastard. You've never been punting on the Thames," I said. "You steal the boat and I'll be so happy to get out of here I'll row by myself."

"Righto." He grinned and was gone.

We lay on our backs in the grass, waiting. There was something odd about the sky, but it didn't occur to me at the moment what it was. I could feel Choy-lin beside me, hear her deep breathing as she rested.

Leigh was breathing deeply, too, and then started to snore very softly. I think I resented him then, but I tried to tell myself it was because some good men had died to get him out of a country he shouldn't have stayed in in the first place. But I knew that Choy-lin had something to do with the way I felt at that moment. It would have been nice to get her off somewhere in a normal setting and court her a little and find out if we could be lovers.

I glanced at her again. She, too, had fallen asleep. I sat up and looked around and listened. I wasn't much of a smoker, but I wanted a cigarette quite badly then.

I heard someone jogging toward us and reached for the Luger, but it was Leslie. "All right," he said. "We've got to hurry."

I shook Choy-lin and Leigh awake. They got up without a word and we hurried after Leslie.

We got down to the edge of the water and followed Leslie to where a small sampan had been pulled up onto the mud. We slipped and splashed and finally got into it, with me shoving us off the bank, getting wet from the thighs down before hoisting myself over the low gunwale into the boat. There were no oarlocks, just a couple of wooden paddles for use where the water was too deep to pole over. Leslie and I took the paddles and started in.

Halfway over I knew we were making very good time, but my arms and shoulders were protesting and my sides ached from leaning over to dig the paddle into the muddy water. I had to rest and said so, and we stopped.

"How'd you get the Queen Mary here?" I asked Leslie.

"Just took it, old boy," he said. "Left the rest of my kip tied up on the pier with the mooring line. Owner will be able to buy three sampans with that. Maybe more."

"You're getting soft in your dotage," I said.

"Look," he pointed. "Current is moving us a bit. Have to go at it again, I'm afraid."

So we did. With every stroke I felt muscles straining and my blood pounding. Just before I would have had to stop no matter what the circumstances, we felt the sampan shudder slightly and slide easily up on the mud. I looked around in relief. Leigh and Choy-lin already were getting out onto the bank. Leslie and I climbed out, starting to get stiff immediately, and dragged the boat onto the shore.

Back across the river was Laos. Nearby, perched on the edge of a bank that dropped sheer into the Mekong, was the town of Nong Khai. All the weariness went out of me in a rush.

We were, at last, back in Thailand. With luck and caution we might make it safely home. We started climbing the rough stone steps up from the nearby boat landing toward the town. We weren't worried about Immigrations and Customs officials just then; it was not quite daylight and they'd still be in bed and we had made no noise crossing the river. What faced us now was the task of getting transportation of any kind, anything at all, to get us south. It was starting to get light.

Then I heard a strange, deep rolling sound. Startled, I looked around but saw nothing unusual. The others paused as I did and while we stood there it came again, a long, booming sound like the surf. Suddenly I knew what was wrong with the sky back there on the river bank. It had been clear for weeks, but when I had lain there looking up, it was starting to cloud over.

Now I looked up just in time to see heavy gray clouds closing out the dawn sky.

"Look," said Choy-lin, pointing back toward Laos.

We could see the driving rain, drumming into the countryside and moving toward the river like a row of gray shields.

There was another booming roll of thunder.

"It's the monsoon," I said.

——————— eight

WE NEEDED A QUICK DECISION; THE NEXT hour could be critical. We huddled under the shed at the top of the stone steps leading up from the riverbank. The shed was an adjunct of the immigration officer's home and office. In less than an hour the entire town of Nong Khai would be up and about, and light sleepers who had heard the thunder might be turning out already. The dogs of the town, all afflicted with mange, were scavenging with the first light but not having much luck.

We had to get south and we had to hurry.

Leslie rubbed the stubble on his chin and gazed thoughtfully at the approaching rain. I looked at it, too, but my senses were starting to become dulled with fatigue and hunger.

"What do you think, Michael?" Leslie asked.

I took my time answering. "We have to get south. We can't use the main road. If we moved east a little, we could hook up on the Friendship Highway and roll right into the Thai army barracks at Lop Buri and on to Bangkok. But we'd run the risk of ambush. So we have to move on secondary roads. In Thailand that means carabao trails, rice paddies, an occasional stretch of pavement. But the monsoon has come like thunder out of China, as the song goes, and we're going to have a hell of a time on roads up here.

"Which leads me to this: if we move off the main roads, we need a jeep. And gasoline and food. Which means we've got to get it right here and damned fast and get started."

Choy-lin turned to me. "You've been here before?"

"Yes," I said. "The Southeast Asia Treaty Organization asked me up once to cover an exercise. Moved all over the area. Then I came back for another exercise two years later and once after that I came up to do a series on the problems of the northeast."

"What do you suggest, Michael?" Leslie asked. I glanced at Leigh, sitting a little apart from us and gazing toward Laos, watching the approaching rain.

"There are several jeeps in town," I said. "One belongs to the Immigration people here. Another belongs to the district commissioner of police. The only other one I know of belongs to the company commander of an army unit stationed about a mile out of town, toward the airstrip. We have to take one of them, and I'd suggest the one owned by Immigration. For one thing, it's bound to be somewhere nearby. If we steal any other one, we'll have the Thai army looking for us. If we take the Immigration one, the cops and the army will spend a little while laughing about it before they get around to searching for it. By that time we'll be halfway to Udon. It's the only way. The one train is too risky and probably won't be able to run anyway because the rains will wash out a bridge or two. The so-called buses sure as hell can't make it, in this weather. Despite all the trouble the rains will cause, it may be the best thing that could happen to us."

"At any rate," Leslie said briskly, "we've got to get moving. Where's the jeep we're going to borrow?"

"Why don't you stay here this time, Les?" I said. "I'll bring the jeep around. I know where he keeps it."

Choy-lin spoke, a little reluctantly. "Can we get some food and a little water? I'm sorry, but I'm famished."

"I'll try," I said. "Wait here."

I moved off around the corner of the shed and looked up the dirt street. Nobody was up yet. The Immigration officer's home was across a small open lot and the jeep was kept behind his home under a small shed. I made it around the corner of his house. A dog came from nowhere, teeth bared and snarling. I kicked at it and it darted away, still snarling. I slipped into the shed and looked at the jeep.

It was an old one, and I thanked God for that. It meant that there was no ignition switch. All you had to do was turn the short lever and step on the starter button just above the accelerator. The jeep had a canvas top but no side curtains. I looked around the shed—it was getting quite light now—and found a full five-gallon can of gasoline. I put it on the floor in the back of the jeep. There was another full can strapped to the left rear of the jeep. I looked again but didn't see anything else that might be of use, so I got in the jeep, held my breath, and stepped on the starter.

It coughed and roared to life and I dropped the gearshift into first and tore out of the shed back to where the others were waiting.

I drove straight across the Immigration officer's front lawn and stopped with a great squeal of brakes. Leslie herded Choy-lin and Leigh into the back and swung into the front seat. Every dog in town converged and went into paroxysms of barking. As I headed the jeep on the street that led away from town I could hear shouting behind us. I glanced in the rearview mirror and saw the same Immigration officer who had been so cordial to me on previous visits. He was running across the lawn, wearing only a pair of shorts, shaking his fist and shouting. The old Vietnam cynicism caught up with me for a split second and I heard myself mutter: Sorry about that.

Now we were committed. The next town of any size was Udon, which wasn't exactly a metropolis but would have food and water. We might have a hell of a time reaching it, though, with the rain right behind us.

"I'm sorry about the food, Choy-lin," I said. "There didn't seem to be any chance in Nong Khai. We'll either buy some rice from a farmer or make a raid in Udon. It might be a while yet, though."

"It's all right," she replied. "Please don't worry about it."

We drove in silence for a while. I was pushing the jeep, getting all the miles in I could before the monsoon caught us. After a half-hour or so Leigh leaned forward and said, quite calmly, "Stop the next time you see either a farmer or a farmhouse. Buy rice, a section of bamboo stalk, and some coconut milk. If you cannot get the milk, buy a coconut. Make sure we have matches. If you cannot buy it, steal it. We must have food. I know what to do with it." Then he leaned back.

Leslie turned in his seat and searched Leigh's face. "Are you feeling better?" he asked.

But it was too late. Leigh laughed uproariously and began to sing in Chinese, imitating the queer, atonal Chinese music scale.

"What the hell," I said. "Let's follow orders and see what happens."

Another half-hour of silence and I spotted a farmer walking beside a water buffalo, the beast pulling a cart loaded with rice. The farmer was on his way to a market somewhere. Roads were so bad they seldom got their products south, where they might get more money. I stopped the jeep and got out, feeling around for the Thai money I was still carrying. I pointed to the rice and held out a handful of baht. The farmer stared at the money and took several of the bills. Then I pointed to the pile of bamboo in the cart and he handed me a section and took another bill. We went through the same ritual with the coconuts. I started to have a healthy respect for Leigh's knowledge of Asia. How had he known the farmer would be marketing these exact three things?

"I have matches," Leslie called from the jeep.

I piled the stuff into the jeep, the uncooked rice wrapped in large, wide leaves, and we went off down the road again. After three or four miles I stopped the jeep off the roadside and turned to Leigh. "It's all yours," I said.

Without a word he climbed out of the jeep and started searching the ground. When we realized he was looking for firewood, we got out to help. Leslie got the fire started and we watched in fascination as Leigh put the rice down in the bamboo stalk, cracked the coconut on the sharp edge of a rock, and poured the milk in with the rice. Then he poured a little of the milk on the ground and stirred up the mud. He filled the open end of the bamboo section with the mud, placed it gently in the fire, and sat down to wait.

"I wish my nanny were here," he said. "She knows songs we could sing." The others happened to be looking away at that moment, but I found myself looking Leigh square in the eye. His eyes were every bit as compelling as I remembered from the photo, but at that moment they were dancing in amusement.

There was a *plopping* sound and I looked down at the bamboo. The fire had cooked the rice in the milk, causing it to expand and forcing the mud out of the end. It was a clever way of keeping the rice from spilling and knowing when it was thoroughly cooked. I had to admire Leigh. Crazy as he was, he knew more about Asian cooking than any of us.

I shook the rice out onto leaves and we ate it with our fingers. It may have been one of the finest meals I've ever had. Certainly it was the most welcome. When we had finished, we kicked out the fire, carefully rewrapped the rest of the uncooked rice in its leaves, and got back into the jeep. Feeling better, we started off again, in high spirits, for Udon.

We had hardly gotten started when the rain caught us.

The first few drops hit my leg from the side. They felt like huge bullets, like dum-dums striking with force behind them. At the same time I heard them spattering on the faded canvas top and saw them hitting the road so hard they were kicking up dust. In a few seconds the rain came from behind and washed over us like floodwaters, cutting visibility down to ten yards or so in front of the jeep. The road, which in spite of the dust had been firm under our wheels, suddenly became treacherous with rivulets of fast-moving water. Nothing could stay dry in that rain, and in minutes all of us were soaked. The rain hammered in through the aging canvas, blew in from the open sides. It was a cold, hard, lashing rain and it whipped at us without mercy as we slipped and slid toward Udon, going much, much slower than before.

"At least," Leslie said cheerfully, "the opposition will be having the same troubles."

"Yeah," I said. "Unless they're waiting comfortably in Udon."

Choy-lin leaned forward. "Is that possible?" she asked.

"I don't know," I said truthfully. "I just don't know."

We talked very little after that. It was difficult handling

the wheel of the jeep and I think the gloom affected all of us. It was very gray, very cold, and very wet. After several hours Leslie took the wheel, with all of us getting out to stretch in spite of the rain. We were wet through anyway.

Late in the afternoon the rain stopped but the skies remained clouded over and the road as much a quagmire as ever. We pushed on, taking turns at the wheel of the jeep into the early evening.

A few miles out of Udon I stopped the jeep to confer with Leslie.

"I want to skirt the town," I said. "I know a way around it. It means sleeping out in the cold and all that, but it may be the wisest thing to do."

Leslie snapped his finger. "I almost forgot," he said. "I pulled a map out of the glove compartment of the Citroen." He found it in an inside pocket. It was wet but legible and we spread it out and looked at it.

"You know the country, Michael," Leslie said. "We'll follow you." Choy-lin nodded and Leigh merely looked uninterested, staring at the countryside.

"Okay, let's try it this way. Udon—or near it—to Khon Kaen. There's a leprosy clinic there where we may be able to scrounge some food and clothes without causing too much of a stir. From there we'll head for Maha Sarakham and on to Korat. I've got a friend near Korat, runs a sawmill up in the teak country. We can rest there and then"—I ran my finger down the map—"make a dash for Bangkok straight on, or swing around by two alternate routes, Prachin Buri, which I don't know very well, or Sara Buri, where I know there's gasoline."

I leaned back and we studied the map.

"Of course," I said. "We won't go by the main road south. If they are as smart as they've been up to now, that route will be watched, especially that great stretch going into Korat, where the road is first-rate."

Leslie nodded. "All right, chum. Lead on."

It took three hours to circle Udon. At one point we could see it quite clearly, a comfortable up-country town with a couple of small but decent hotels. There would be dry beds, food, drink. Civilization. But I kept the jeep pointing south and we got around it and went weaving down the slippery mud of side roads.

And the man we were doing this for hadn't spoken in hours.

It began to rain again.

We stopped for the night at a small country shrine. Thailand is dotted with them, coated with brilliant paint on the outside and almost bare inside. Ours was a small shrine but dry. The floor was worn smooth with the bare feet of the peasants who came here to pray. We were sure nobody would be out on a night like this one, and we were right. I pulled the jeep around where it would be hidden from the road and Choy-lin went out and found some dry wood under the steps leading to the shrine. We built a small fire inside on the wooden floor, watching it carefully, and cooked the rest of the rice. Leslie raised the possibility of dysentery, but we said the hell with it; we had bigger problems.

"We'll split up the night watches, Michael," Leslie said.

"Do you really think they're necessary?"

"We just can't take chances."

"All right," I said. "I'll take the first half."

The three of them stretched out on the bare floor, Choy-lin in the middle and all getting close for warmth. I walked around them and sat near the entrance of the shrine. I looked up but couldn't see the tower roof of even this small shrine. It was pitch dark, at first. After a while I got my night vision and could see outside a little, but not very much.

The first hour went by slowly, the second just as slow. Leslie got up to go outside and relieve himself, grunting "coconut milk" at me as he passed. He went back in and was asleep almost at once. I followed his example and sat down just inside the shrine again.

When my chin bumped suddenly against my chest, I snapped my head back up and grabbed the Luger in a near-panic. I had dozed off, but there was nothing out there in the night that meant danger.

To help me stay awake I started thinking about Thailand, about the northeast.

It was the poorest section of the country and the most embattled.

The soil was poor. Villages were isolated in the rainy season and farmers had trouble getting any crops to market. The rice yield was the lowest in the nation. In a nation three-quarters covered by forests, the northeast was flat, almost bare, poor and backward. The people were backward, too, but it wasn't their fault. I'd guessed there were some ten million of them in the northeast, including a lot of Vietnamese who wandered away from the shooting years ago and just settled on land nobody else happened to be using. The rest of the people mostly were of Lao stock. It showed up in their language and the Reds used it to their advantage: they distributed radios to a lot of villagers and the radios were fixed-band receivers tuned on either Radio Peking or Radio Hanoi.

The message they got was very clever. It didn't exhort them to become Communists. Instead it played on their Lao ancestry, urging them to secede and become a part of Laos. The part of Laos controlled by Souvannavong and his Pathet Lao Communists, of course. It also hammered away with the idea that Bangkok was a long way south and traditionally unconcerned with the peoples of the northeast. There was a time when that was undoubtedly true, but there had been changes in the old kingdom of Siam. Young King Phumiphon and his lovely queen visited the northeast as often as possible. They really were making an effort to show the farmers that Thailand was a nation, with a national purpose and a national destiny. I believed it, too. For me Thailand was a bright spot in the rather gloomy picture of Southeast Asia.

You can have it, though, during the monsoon. Especially in the northeast. It was getting to be a long night.

Leigh got up suddenly and went outside. When he came back, he paused and looked down at me. I couldn't see his face, but I had the feeling he wanted to say something, but before I could speak, he moved away and a little while later I heard his soft snore.

At 2 A.M. I walked over and nudged Leslie. He came awake at once and stood up and stretched. I pointed to the luminous dial of my watch and he nodded and walked over to sit where I had been sitting. It was getting very chill and our clothes were still wet; there was no way to dry them. I lay down beside Choy-lin and Leigh. Tired as I was, I had trouble going to sleep just then.

How would it end?

I thought of Uthanipan. For him it ended with a gunshot on the edge of a klong. Before that, though, he had been broken. I was sure he had been very tough. How had they broken him? I thought of his wife and children. Perhaps it had been that way. It was a distressing thought and I rolled over on the hard floor and tried to forget it. Choy-lin whimpered once in her sleep and moved closer to me for warmth.

I felt her head pushed up against my back and I smiled in the darkness.

I heard the rain begin again, hitting the wooden sides of the shrine and blowing in the quickening wind through the entrance. I heard Leslie shift his position, moving farther back into the shrine to get out of the blowing rain.

After a while I fell asleep and slept the rest of the night.

When dawn came, I opened my eyes and sat up.

I felt exactly the way I'd expected after a night in wet clothes on a hard floor. In spite of all the water around, I was thirsty and starting to get hungry again. I looked over at Leslie. He looked haggard but as handsome as ever and he was smiling at me. Choy-lin and Leigh slept on.

Outside the shrine was a sea of mud. Water was standing in the fields and on the roads. It wasn't raining, but the sky was leaden.

I pressed the button on the left side of the Luger and the clip slid out of the handle. Even the gun was wet and would rust eventually if I couldn't find a way to clean it. I looked at the clip; the shells seemed dry enough. I hoped the gun would work if I needed it.

I hoped I wouldn't need it.

I put the clip back and walked out to the jeep, the mud making a sucking noise as my feet went in and pulled out. It was slow walking. I scraped off my shoes on the jeep's small step and got in and tried the engine.

It wouldn't start.

I swore at it.

Leslie walked over. "What's wrong with it?"

"Nothing mechanical," I said. "The damned wiring is wet. I saw it happen up here before with the SEATO people. They can't seem to keep the engines dry."

I got out and raised the hood. Leslie and I took out handkerchiefs, none too dry themselves, and started wiping the wires. We had been at it several minutes when Choy-lin called from the steps of the shrine, "Mr. Hawkins!"

I looked up and got a jolt.

There were perhaps a dozen of them, stocky, peasant types, wearing old clothing and canvas sneakers and the conical hats of the farmers. They were as ragged and dirty as any poor rice farmer in the northeast.

But the guns they carried were clean and modern and the

few bandoleers of ammunition slung over shoulders looked deadly enough.

I glanced around. There were two more of them at the back of the shrine. Leslie was standing quite still, counting them to himself and probably wondering who they were. I thought I knew.

At that moment Leigh walked out of the shrine and sat down on the steps.

Nobody moved or spoke for a few minutes. I decided to take the initiative.

"Anybody speak English?" I asked.

No answer.

Leslie spoke to them in French.

No answer.

I put my hands together and gave them the traditional Thai greeting.

They merely stared.

Then one of them barked a command. I thought he spoke in Lao, but I couldn't be sure. Before the sound of his voice died, two of them ran up the steps of the shrine. They went through the entrance low and against the wall, not missing a thing, then called back to the man who had spoken and he motioned them back down the steps.

The leader had an automatic rifle in his arms. It looked like a Danish Mattsen, and how he got his hands on it I'd never start to guess. Now he used it to motion us over to the steps, and Leslie and I trudged over and stood by Choy-lin and Leigh. There was another command and two more of them went over and looked down at the jeep's engines. Then one of them climbed inside and tried the starter.

"That's going to be a great disappointment to him," I said to no one in particular.

But I was wrong. The damned thing started.

The leader's face split in a wide grin. He scampered over and dropped the hood of the jeep and fastened it down, then ordered his man out from behind the wheel. The leader sat there for a few minutes, racing the motor and smiling, the Mattsen slung over his shoulder.

Abruptly he stopped smiling and turned off the motor. Swinging down out of the jeep, he walked up to the steps and called up to us, his voice harsh. Then he started shaking his finger at us, a terrible violation of Thai manners. We couldn't understand a word he was saying, but the tone wasn't very friendly.

I began to get annoyed and I had reached the point where I felt we had nothing to lose anyway, so I yelled back at him, "Shut up, you silly bastard."

It took him by surprise, but only for a second. He came hurrying up the steps and stuck his face into mine, climbing a couple of steps higher so we'd be on the same level. He roared at me. His breath was terrible, and he went on for perhaps a minute and a half at the top of his lungs. When he stopped, his eyes were flashing and his chin was jutting just a few inches away.

I gave it right back to him: "Keep your Goddamned hands off my jeep," I yelled. "Take your private army and get the hell out of here or I'll break your scrawny neck." Then I swore a little and found to my surprise that I was more than annoyed; I was getting mad.

Leslie sensed it, too. "I say, Michael, old boy," he said calmly. "Hate to get shot this late in the game." But I didn't answer him. I was in a staring contest with the leader. We held each other's eyes for a few seconds and without looking away the leader slowly reached up and clutched the sling of the Mattsen and took the gun from his shoulder. I heard him work the bolt, sliding a shell up into the chamber. I heard the safety go off and felt a taste of copper under my tongue and the blood draining from my face. But I held his eye. It was the only thing I could think to do. I couldn't have gotten the Luger out in time.

Suddenly he rammed the muzzle of the Mattsen into my stomach. It hurt like hell, but I stood still and watched his eyes. To my astonishment I saw them crinkle at the corners as a wide smile spread over his face. He started to laugh, taking the gun away and putting the safety back on and slinging it over his shoulder. His laughter grew and he started slapping me on the shoulder, laughing uproariously, and the rest of the band joined in. I managed what I hoped was a dignified smile.

From out of nowhere I heard Leigh suddenly start to laugh, too.

The leader stopped as abruptly as he started. He turned his back on me and walked down the steps and huddled with three or four of the band, but I noticed that someone kept an eye—and a gun—on us all the time. Then the leader was back and gesturing us back inside the shrine, pointing to the sky. It was going to rain again soon.

We filed inside and the band surrounded us and sat on the floor, their backs to the wall. We stood in the center for a few minutes and the leader came in and gestured again and we sat down.

We sat in silence. We obviously were waiting for something, but I had no idea what it would be. They were unpredictable as hell.

Leslie turned to me. "Who are they?" he asked.

"Bandits," I said.

"Bandits?" repeated Choy-lin.

"Yes. The northeast is full of them. They start out as opium smugglers and end up stealing whatever they think they can use. The Communists have been trying to use them for years, but the bandits treasure their independence. They're the despair of the Thai police."

"Are they . . . murderers?" she asked.

"I'm sure they've killed before," I said.

"What will they do with us?"

"I haven't the slightest idea."

"Hope you don't lose your temper again, old man," Leslie said. "You rather gave me a fright back there. I thought Pancho Villa here was going to shoot you."

Before I could answer, two more bandits came in carrying a wicker basket between them. They set it on the floor of the shrine and started taking out smaller baskets wrapped in dirty cloth. As they unwrapped the small baskets I realized they were about to offer us breakfast.

Seconds later the leader had handed us chopsticks and, smiling broadly, he pushed the food toward us. We nodded and dug in. There was rice, and cucumbers served in a dark red sauce, fish of some sort, and something I had to be hungry to eat—fried cicadas.

We ate without speaking, the leader joining us. The rest of the band had eaten or would eat later. They merely waited, ringing the walls, until we finished. Leslie grumbled under his breath and ate only rice. Choy-lin ate very daintily, with most of the men watching her in open admiration. She looked fresh and pretty for all she'd been through, and the still-damp clothes clinging to her outlined the perfectly proportioned form inside them. Leigh ate heartily and quickly and then drew his knees up and hid his face again. The bandit leader gave him a curious glance and ignored him.

When we had finished, the same two bandits came back and cleared away the food baskets. The leader stood up. We were about to reach the most dangerous moment—they were going to leave, and what would they do with us?

We got another wide smile from the leader and he made an odd little bow, bending from the waist and jerking upright quickly. With him leading, the bandits filed out of the shrine and down the steps.

They were going to leave us unharmed. They hadn't even searched us.

They trooped down the steps as the first few raindrops started. The leader plunged through the mud and over to the jeep. My heart sank as he got in behind the wheel and yelled happily. Several others piled into the jeep just as he got it started.

He knew how to handle it, all right; he checked to see if it were in four-wheel drive, then pulled the gearshift into first and moved slowly out toward the road, with the rest of the band trudging along beside the jeep. He swung the jeep onto the muddy road, paused to look back at us standing on the steps, and smiled again. He beeped the horn twice and, still grinning, drove slowly away with the bandits following.

We stood there a long time, watching them until they topped a small hill and dropped out of sight on the other side.

"Damn," I said with fervor.

"What shall we do now?" Choy-lin asked.

"Look at the map," I said.

The rain was starting in earnest, so we went back into the shrine and spread the map on the floor.

We couldn't go back and we couldn't stay. In Udon we'd be the center of attention. Back in Nong Khai the Immigration people would want to talk with us. If we delayed, the other side would have time not only to set up watches for us in the south but to start a sweep north to search for us. We had no chance at all if we were caught out here in the country. The bandits could have shot all of us and our bodies might never have been found. Our survival lay in not being where we were supposed to be, in doing the unexpected but at the same time keeping on the move and working south.

Three of us discussed it, with Leigh sitting nearby and

humming to himself, laughing quietly now and then. We reached a decision.

"We've got to get to Khon Kaen," I said. "We might get help at the leprosy clinic."

"How far?" Choy-lin asked.

"I'd say about fifty or sixty miles."

She thought it over. "And we must walk?" she asked.

"Unless we can get our hands on another jeep or some means of transportation."

Leslie grinned. "That's the trouble with you Americans," he said. "You want everything automated."

"Have you got a better idea?" I asked him.

"But of course, old boy."

"All right, I'm listening."

"When in Rome and all that," he said. "We'll simply buy or steal a water buffalo and a cart."

I looked at him in frank admiration, then mentally kicked myself for being so stupid not to think of it myself.

"Hell, yes," I said. "Let's get started."

nine

IN THE END WE HAD TO STEAL A BUFFALO. We had emptied our pockets of baht, but it wasn't nearly enough to buy a water buffalo and a cart, even if we could find one for sale. So we kept back a little baht to buy food with later on, if necessary, stuck the rest under a rock on a farmer's porch and took his buffalo and cart. I was a little surprised we'd gotten away with it, but then the Thai people are a trusting lot. Even in the northeast.

There was room for one person to sit at the front of the cart, feet propped against the braces of the yoke, and drive. Driving consisted of swatting the buffalo with a long, thin bamboo strip every time it showed an inclination to stop, which was about twice a minute.

Leslie drove in the beginning, with the rest of us bouncing

in the cart and trying to hold on to the sides so the jolts wouldn't be as sharp in the rutted road. It was actually better because of the mud's softening effect on the road, but still it left a lot to be desired. On top of that, the cart still smelled of night soil and fermented coconut milk and God knows what else. I didn't care. By midday we were ten or twelve miles closer to Khon Kaen, even moving off the roads and crossing the fields where possible, playing it safe.

After a while we got off on a fairly smooth stretch of open country. There was an occasional stand of tall trees and underbrush, alive with cobras and kraits (I was sure), and we detoured around them. The country was flat. The entire northeast pretty much dropped down and led into an alluvial plain in central Thailand and we still were, by my guess, nearly one hundred miles above the spine of mountains that came jutting across the land near Korat. I had a lot of hopes for Korat, providing the sawmill was still in operation and my old friend Boon Song hadn't gotten smashed by any of his elephants. They became rogues sometimes and he had to shoot them, and it was a dangerous thing to have to do.

But we were a long way from Korat.

With the country flattening out and the bouncing reduced considerably, we began to get drowsy with the movement of the cart and the creak of the wheels. One by one we dropped off to sleep.

The rain woke us up again an hour or so later. There was nothing to be done about it, so we hunched up in the cart while it swept over us. I could hear Leslie curse once when it started; then he too hunched his shoulders, turned up his collar, and got soaked along with us.

I swapped places with Leslie and we plodded along through the day, wet and miserable. As darkness approached we held a conference and decided to keep going through the night. The water buffalo was surefooted enough, and Choy-lin volunteered to take turns driving. There was no real reason not to keep moving and every reason why we should.

The rain stopped just before dark. Leslie sat up front again and we moved on, going around a small village that the map showed to be Ban Nam Phong.

Sometime in the night I heard Leslie and Choy-lin trade places. Later on I felt the cart stop. Drowsily I decided that Choy-lin was going off to relieve herself, and I fell asleep again.

What jerked me upright was a bellow of pain and the lurching of the cart. Pure reflex took me straight up and off the end of the cart. I landed on my feet in the mud, struggling to reach the Luger and trying desperately to see.

I heard Choy-lin's cry of despair and headed around front, Leslie and Leigh awake and right behind me. When I could see a little better I noticed two things: our buffalo slumped to the ground, its back left leg twisted and undoubtedly broken, and Choy-lin, sobbing, holding a long, thick length of bamboo.

I was close enough to see the tears in Choy-lin's great, dark eyes. "I'm so sorry," she sobbed. "I'm so sorry."

"What happened?" I asked.

"The cart got stuck," she said. "I tried to pry it loose with the bamboo pole I found, but"—she started crying again—"it slipped somehow. I felt it slip free just as the buffalo moved. I'm so sorry."

Leslie and I bent down and looked at the buffalo. The bamboo must have caught it at just the right moment; the leg was broken and ugly, twisted unnaturally with the end of the broken bone poking jaggedly through the hide. The buffalo lay on its side, still yoked to the cart with one side of the wooden yoke splintered by the buffalo's great weight as it fell. The buffalo's breath was fast and shallow.

"A lot of pain," I said. "We'll have to shoot it. Then we start walking again, damn it."

"Mr. Hawkins, Michael—what can I say?"

"Oh, hell, it's all right," I told her. "You couldn't help it."

"I wanted to help," she said, and looked like she was going to cry again. To stop her as much as anything else I said brusquely, "Let's go. We can't stay here all night."

"Righto," Leslie agreed. "Let's move on."

"You go ahead," I told them. "Move out and I'll catch up with you in a few minutes."

"You'll end it, Michael?" asked Leslie.

"Yes."

They walked off in the direction of Khon Kaen and I squatted down to take another look at the leg. It could never be repaired. There were plenty of buzzards up-country here; I couldn't leave it to die under their ugly beaks. I moved around to the buffalo's head. It's breath was still fast and labored. One great brown eye gazed at me and I couldn't look at it again.

"Oh, hell," I said, and got out the Luger and shot it in the head.

Before the sound died, I was walking away from it. I caught up with the other three and we trudged wearily down what had been a narrow, dirt road and now was more like a creek bed.

"If we hurry," I grumbled, "we can be in Khon Kaen by morning."

Damn Leigh, I thought. Damn everybody. But especially Leigh. We seemed to be going to a hell of a lot of trouble to get a lunatic to safety.

"Christ," I grumbled.

"What?" asked Leslie.

"Nothing," I said. And we kept walking.

The towns of northeast Thailand are like beads on a string, with plenty of string between each one. The towns are spaced exactly the distance a water buffalo can pull a cart of rice to market and return the next day. There is no reason for the towns except for the markets, and there was little else other than the markets and a few stores and a regional police station.

Khon Kaen was different in that it had one other reason for being; it contained a clinic where lepers were treated, and there were an estimated hundred thousand lepers in the northeast. A lot of them ended up in Khon Kaen for treatments at the clinic, but by the time they made up their minds to go there, it usually was too late to do them any good. The clinic itself was a miracle of persistence. I had visited it once before to do a story. It was run by two white doctors and was a part of the Maranatha Bible School, also in Khon Kaen, and supported by both the Christian and Missionary Alliance and the American Leprosy Mission. The doctors, I recalled, had to negotiate with seventeen different farmers to buy the necessary land for the clinic. With the Thai love of bargaining, the negotiations went on for the better part of a year. Then the Thai government refused to give the doctors permission to build a hospital. I don't know why. The doctors got around it by building a "clinic" and adding "recovery rooms" until they had a full-blown hospital, which they always referred to as the clinic. They operated on a wooden table without lighting. They lived at the clinic and ran the risk of becoming lepers themselves. But they wouldn't leave and their courage and persistence won the admiration of the entire northeast.

Now it was the mission I headed for; I was sure the doctors would remember me and I hoped to get food and transportation. So when we reached the outskirts of Khon Kaen at dawn, I left the others resting in a stand of trees and made my way across the small curved bridge, crossed the grounds of the clinic and over to where the house rose a few feet off the ground on stilts, like all Thai houses in the northeast.

I went up the steps and hesitated before knocking on the door. There was no one else around that I could see. Finally I knocked and heard footsteps inside.

The door swung open and I looked down into the mild blue eyes of Dr. Ludkins.

"Hello, Doctor," I said. "Remember me?"

His cherubic face beamed back at me, a ruddy, pleasant face under crew-cut white hair, with kind eyes behind rimless glasses. "Of course, of course, Michael Hawkins. Come in, come in, come in."

I stepped inside and got the first feeling of peace and security I'd had in weeks. The house was just as I remembered it.

There was a battered piano and a sturdy teak table and reproductions of several Old Masters around the walls, and a row of whiskey glasses gleaming on a small bar. It gleamed with the warmth of polished wood and a deep, comfortable couch and a woven rug. The whole impression was of warmth and peace, and as I stood looking at it I felt very tired suddenly, and wanted nothing more than a bath and a civilized drink with Dr. Ludkins and some decent food. And safety.

He was studying me. "You need some dry clothes and a little food, don't you? You look like you might have a fever. You sit here on the couch and let me fix you up, eh?"

"Where's Dr. Marston?" I asked, slumping gratefully on the couch.

"Took the train into Bangkok for some DDS pills. We're getting low."

"Doctor, there's something I have to tell you. I'm not alone and I'm in trouble. We need help."

"I know," he said.

"You know?"

"Yes." He sat in a chair across from me and reached for his thick, curved pipe. He fired it up before speaking again and puffed on it as he spoke.

"Two days ago we had other visitors. They were strangers. Three Orientals. I'd say two Lao and one either Vietnamese or Chinese. They came here and asked if we'd seen any other strangers in Khon Kaen. We told them no, but they went through the wards, looking at our patients, and not being very polite about it, either.

"Finally they went out back and looked for the old Land Rover, but Marston was out in town with it. They asked me how many vehicles there were in town. I told them our Land Rover and the three or four police jeeps. They asked a couple of other questions about towns and roads and how long I expected the rains to last. Then they left. They didn't even say thanks."

"They aren't very friendly, Dr. Ludkins."

"I can believe it," he said. "When I opened the door and saw you standing there, I suddenly got the feeling it might have been you they were looking for." He peered at me quizzically over his glasses and drew on the pipe.

"It is," I admitted. "And three others with me. We've got to go south without getting caught. I can't tell you any more than that." I paused. "Will you help us?"

I waited while he fumbled with the pipe again.

"I won't ask you," he said, "what's going on. I don't want to know. I know a lot of things are happening up here in the northeast, a lot of political things with all these Chinese radios and the Pathet Lao propaganda. And more opium-growing than ever. And bandits. And now you." He blew smoke into a long line toward the ceiling. "You're probably in a hurry, son. Let's get together whatever you need."

"You won't like it," I warned. "I need some decent food in a kit of some sort, and some dry clothes, enough for four people. And one more thing."

"I know," he sighed. "You'll need the Land Rover."

We got the food and clothing together. Dr. Ludkins threw in a bottle of Scotch and a few packs of Dr. Marston's cigarettes. He stuffed an old musette bag full of food and a bottle of water and we walked out together to the Land Rover.

He patted it on the fender. "Take care of her," he said. "She's invaluable up here."

I promised him a fleet of them if we got out all right. Then I asked him not to mention we'd been there, swore I'd never forget his kindness, and drove off toward the outskirts of Khon Kaen. I left him standing outside the house, his face wreathed in smoke from the pipe. All the way out of town I felt overwhelmed by his generosity. But that wasn't all I felt.

The enemy camp had been there, too. They were somewhere in front of us and we'd have to be even more cautious now. When they didn't find us in the south, they'd start over, and somehow we had to slip through them. The most important thing was to keep moving.

Move we did, and in style.

In clothes that were ill-fitting but dry, warmed by food and buoyed by a quick dash of Scotch, we sat in the comfort of a covered vehicle, dry and cheerful as the sturdy Land Rover churned through the mud, bearing us south.

"You're starting to get quite a beard there," Leslie said, smiling.

"So are you," I said. "And Leigh. Even Choy-lin."

I heard her soft laugh from the back seat of the Land Rover. When I glanced in the rearview mirror, I saw her running her fingers through her hair and examining her rough, men's clothing with a critical eye.

"I look terrible," she said.

"You could step onto any dance floor in the world and be the center of attention," I said, meaning it.

She smiled at me. "You're a flirt, Mr. Hawkins."

"I thought we all got on a first-name basis sometime back."

"You're a flirt, Michael."

"Terrible, isn't he?" said Leslie. "It's this way everywhere we go."

"Have you known each other long?" she asked.

"Too long," I grunted.

And happy, and teasing each other, we came to Maha Sarakham.

It is the principal town in the province of the same name. Like the others, it boasts a marketplace. Like the others, the buildings are all one- and two-story structures of mud bricks and wood and straw thatching. Some of them had corrugated tin roofing that made a tremendous clanging sound in the monsoon rain.

I stopped the Land Rover on the edge of town.

"Well," I said. "What do you think?"

"What's ahead?" Leslie asked, and we got out the map again.

"Borabu, a good-sized town. Then villages. Ban Phai, Phon. A hell of a bad road beyond Phon, as I recall. Then more villages. Here, on the map—Ban Wang Muang, Ban Talet Khae, Ban Choho.

"And after that," I said, "there's Korat and a measure of security. Then the sprint to Bangkok."

"All right," Leslie mused. "If they're ahead of us, as you say, then where do you think they'll hole up? They can't stay in every market town in the northeast. And our problem is outwitting them, all right, but not knocking about up-country any longer than necessary."

I tried to think. "They'll watch the roads. We know that. But when it isn't raining, the visibility is so good and the ground so flat we can see for miles. They can't have anything faster than the Land Rover, or I don't think they can. I say let's go like hell as long as we can see, and when we can't, either hide and wait or make a hell of a circle. We've got plenty of gas."

"But staying out of towns as much as possible," Choy-lin said.

"Yes."

Leslie pulled the Scotch out and when Choy-lin shook her head, he handed the bottle to me. I took a long pull at it and watched him do the same before putting it back.

"Now," he said. "What about this one?"

"Straight through," I said. "It would be hell getting around this one. I know the roads here pretty well. It's the middle of the day and most people will be indoors at lunch or taking a nap. The main street is a long one, but wide, and you can see the other end. Nobody can spring anything here. What do you say?"

Leslie nodded and I started the motor and headed right down the middle of town, remembering to drive on the left. There were only a few people on the street, stopping to watch the Land Rover pass by. I noted that there had been a fire. Part of the old market had burned. The rest of the town was just as I remembered it, a town trying bravely to be a provincial capital, even to the extent of a few splashes of paint here and there. It took less than ten minutes to get out the other side and into the country again.

Halfway to Borabu I stopped the Land Rover and we got out. Choy-lin walked off by herself, heading for the brush, and Leslie sauntered across the road for the bushes on the other side.

The moment they got out of sight, Leigh's hand fell heavily on my shoulder and I spun around.

His eyes were lit with excitement but quite sane. "Don't say anything," he whispered, words tumbling swiftly after each other in an English upper-class accent all the years in China hadn't erased. "I've got to see you alone. I need time to talk with you. Don't tell the others, either one of them. I've decided to trust you. Now you've got to trust me."

His hand tightened on my shoulder. "You've got to help me," he added. "You've got to."

Before I could react, Choy-lin stepped out of the brush and started toward us. Leigh's hand dropped swiftly and his eyes resumed the vacant look of disinterest we had come to expect.

Leslie came up and we smoked and stretched and got back into the Land Rover.

The miles rolled by.

Sixteen miles to Borabu; we doglegged around it because it was easy to do, and kept moving, feeling very good about the miles behind us. Twenty-seven miles later we went straight through Ban Phai because there was no other way to get beyond it. Leigh sang at least halfway to Phon. He sang in Mandarin and Choy-lin joined in occasionally, singing in a soft, quavering voice, and Leigh seemed pleased. Then he stopped in midsong abruptly and turned to gaze in silence out the window. Choy-lin and Leslie exchanged despairing glances.

We got to Phon with no trouble and bore down on Song Hong. Somewhere near Song Hong we had stopped some many days before for the helicopter to be refueled. I wondered what had happened to the helicopter and its crew. I wondered what had happened to Sinn.

What happened, what happened . . .

You could grow very weary counting up our casualties, and trying to figure out where it all began. It was impossible to say it began with my meeting Leigh in Korea, years ago. Or even before that, with the two of us on opposite sides of the Atlantic, deciding to become newsmen (or more accurately in my case, drifting into journalism out of boredom with everything else).

Destiny, fate. I kicked around the idea of an orderly universe and had to smile. What booted the earth along was the sudden turn, the coincidence, the words blurted out for no reason at all, the friendship between unlikely individuals. Doing something for no good reason just for the hell of it. That's how things started, really.

But how did they end?

I couldn't even guess.

Five or six miles out of Ban Wang Muang we ran into a road so treacherous with mud and cart ruts we had to take it in first gear, and I was too busy to think of anything else. Just when we got past the worst of it, another cloudburst caught us and we had to stop the Land Rover on the side of the road and wait for the rain to end.

After it stopped, Leslie took the wheel and we wrestled on again, all of us getting tired now. Choy-lin was getting little lines of fatigue around her eyes, but she tried bravely to smile, and to keep our spirits up we talked for a while about nonimportant things. We were starting to have a rapport.

There was nothing but fields on both sides of Ban Wang Muang, so we went down the middle, Leslie driving and me searching for other vehicles in the streets and watching closely the second-story windows in the few larger buildings.

Then we were through it and I relaxed, putting my head on the back of the seat.

In the back of my mind, ever since our last stop, there had been a thought growing, with me denying it, then considering it again, then pushing it away. Now it was back and stronger and instead of just an isolated feeling it began to assert itself, and finally I came to believe it.

Leigh wasn't crazy.

————————— ten

THERE WAS A TRUMPETING IN MY EAR. I opened my eyes and sat up, startled.

The first thing I saw was an elephant.

I blinked and looked again and saw several of them. They were swaying down the side of the road a mere ten yards from the Land Rover. Leslie and Choy-lin were standing outside, Choy-lin laughing and clasping her hands in delight. I glanced around; Leigh was still in the Land Rover, but he was watching them, too.

It took me a few blinks to adjust, but after I got a quick look around, I felt a lot better.

For the first time in days there were mountains around us, covered in forests. The elephants, I knew, were tame ones used to pull the teak logs down from these mountains to the sawmills. The Land Rover was parked on the edge of a wonderfully smooth, paved road. The air was cooler with the higher altitude and, best of all, the skies were only partly cloudy and the humidity seemed lower. The country was familiar and I began to feel very good about it.

Leslie turned and saw I was awake. "Hallo, Michael," he called happily. "Have a look. Aren't they magnificent?" He waved toward the elephants.

"They're beautiful animals," Choy-lin said, laughing.

"Yeah," I said, getting out of the Land Rover. "And I think I know who owns them, too."

"Our map says we're near Nakhon Ratchasima," Leslie said. "Must be a good-sized place, by the size of the lettering on the map."

"That's Korat," I said. "If I remember correctly, you've been on a paved road for quite a few miles. See anything?"

"No," he answered, and added, "There didn't seem to be any secondary roads. Maybe it was risky, but it seemed the only way."

It was. The roads in this area all led off to sawmills or down to the rain-swollen rivers, where elephants were led at the end of the day to bathe in the muddy water. All of the roads were dead ends.

"We may have outrun the monsoon," I told them. "For a little while at least. Notice how much cooler it is?"

The elephants plodded by, each led by a young Thai who stared at us in frank curiosity.

"Did you just pass what looks like a big country estate, on the left a few miles back?" I asked.

"Yes," said Leslie.

"Okay," I said. "I know where we are. Pretty soon now we'll come to a large shrine on the right of the road. Just past it is a dirt road leading off toward the river and crossing a small wooden bridge. Past the bridge is a sawmill. Let's head for that. The owner is an old friend. We can rest a bit and clean up and figure out the run to Bangkok."

We got back in and started up, with me driving, feeling wonderfully refreshed after a long sleep and because there was no rain and the air was cooler. For the first time I began to feel that nothing would go wrong from here on out, that we would make it. And I looked forward to seeing Boon Song again.

Boon Song was a tough young Thai intellectual. He'd worked in the teak forests as a child. His mother had died of what he later believed was malaria, and his father was killed in a logging accident in these same mountains, not far away. He looked around him and realized he would either be a laborer forever or he'd have to go away to school.

He told me that rather casually one night, but I knew how much guts it took. To get into Thai university in those days you needed patronage, political influence, royal blood, or money. Boon Song had none of those things, but he could read and write and had a great deal of determination. He put together all the baht he could and went down to Chulalongkorn University. I don't know how he did it, but he talked himself in and when he wasn't in school, he worked. He attended school in the morning. In the afternoons he drove a sam lor, a bicycle taxi, and at night he worked as a porter in one of the large hotels. He may have smuggled a bit on the side; I don't know.

I know that he came out of the university with two strong desires: to get himself out of economic bondage, and to help the poor, rural Thais. Armed with his university certificate and an intimate knowledge of teak and elephants, he came north again. He borrowed money and started his own sawmill.

What happened after that was the kind of story all too rare in Asia, and after I had met him, I was happy to write a series about his achievement. The sawmill lost money the first two years, chiefly because Boon Song tripled everybody's wages, opened a communal kitchen and hired cooks to buy and serve decent food, opened a small clinic with a part-time doctor, and started a school. The third year he bought new equipment and automated as much as possible. Nobody lost jobs, because it took men to run the machinery. What it meant was there was more leisure time for Thais who were accustomed to working from sunup to sundown. With their leisure time, Boon Song urged—he didn't force—them to get into the school.

In the fourth year the sawmill's profits were higher than anyone dared dream. Boon Song got married, expanded the business, and sent two bright young Thais to college in Bangkok.

The whole operation snowballed. Boon Song found himself getting rich in spite of the way he used his money. He founded an orphanage and suddenly found himself with two French priests as teachers. Now he had a community of perhaps five thousand persons, living in a clean and happy little settlement in the jungle. The Thai government gave him some sort of decoration for achievement and his wife gave him a succession of round, happy babies. Through all of this he managed to learn English and French and when I saw him last, more than a year before, he was thinking about visiting America.

I'd guessed his age at thirty-five or so.

I was anxious to see him again. He had a good, quick mind, disciplined in business and then as relaxed and gay socially as the average Thai.

I started telling the others about Boon Song, and by the time I finished, I could see the spires of the shrine a mile or so away. We were getting close.

I searched in the rearview mirror for Choy-lin's eyes to tell her she could rest and relax very soon. But I found something else.

"There's a jeep behind us, Leslie," I said. "Coming up fast."

"All right, chum. What do you think?"

"Thai police use Land Rovers up here. It could be one of the civilian SEATO jeeps the engineers use. Or it could be our opposition, showing themselves at last."

"All right. We can bluff it out, and hope. Or we can hide."

I stepped down hard on the accelerator. "I know one thing," I said. "I'm not leading them to Boon Song's place. Maybe we can outrun them."

The shrine flashed by on the right; I ignored the runoff to the sawmill and watched the speedometer needle start climbing. In the mirror I could see the jeep was the same distance back. They would have to be going all-out to keep the gap as narrow as it was. No SEATO engineer would be that interested in us.

"It's them," I said. "We'd better come up with an idea."

"Can you see how many there are in the jeep?" Choy-lin asked, her voice calm. Leigh hadn't stirred.

"No," I replied. "Dr. Ludkins said there had been three of them at the leprosy clinic in Khon Kaen. I think we'd better assume there are at least three now. We're a bit outgunned, wouldn't you say, Leslie?"

He didn't answer. He had the map out and was sweeping it with his eyes. Finally he said, "Rather long run into any cities where we might hide, isn't it?"

"Yep," I said. "The cities aren't all that safe, anyway."

"If we could keep the distance, could we make it into Bangkok?"

"No. There's a problem with the gas. There's only a little left in the drum on the back and we'd have to stop to pour it in."

Choy-lin called from the back seat, "They're getting closer."

I glanced up in the mirror. They were, too. We were in a hell of a fix now. Then my eyes caught something on the road ahead and I felt the first faint stirrings of hope.

"Maybe we can split up and confuse them," Leslie said.

"No," I said, and started to grin. "Help is on the way. The Union Cavalry is just galloping over the ridge."

"I don't understand——" began Choy-lin.

"Up ahead," I said. "Largest police academy in northeast Thailand. And it looks like graduation day." I eased up on the accelerator. If we timed it right, we had a chance, a very good chance.

I could see the jeep quite clearly now. There were three men in it and it was closing fast. I held the Land Rover at a creeping twenty-five miles an hour, my eyes locked on the activity at the police academy. I could see long lines of police cadets at attention and off to one side in front of them, several people seated on a raised platform, and parallel to them, a band.

Leslie had his automatic out. I glanced at him and he gave me a cool, confident smile. "I don't know what you're planning, old boy, but if anything goes wrong, I'm going to get off a few bangs before they pick us up."

"They're very close now," said Choy-lin.

"Here we go," I said. "Get down in the back seat and hang on."

I wrenched the steering wheel and we went off the road, bounced twice, and bore down on the police academy. I could hear the blaring of the band and heard it give a sort of bleat of surprise as I swung the Land Rover straight toward the platform.

The band scattered. I just had time to see people leaping off the platform before glancing in the mirror again to see if the jeep was following. It was right behind us.

I stepped hard on the accelerator again and the Land Rover tore up the middle of the parade ground, raising dust and scattering the officers standing in front of the cadets.

Now was the critical moment. When we reached the end of the row of cadets, I swung the Land Rover around and started back the way we came. We passed the jeep going the other way, not more than six feet apart. I got a glimpse of three startled faces, then tore my eyes away to concentrate on the next problem: getting out.

There were two shots. Warning shots, I prayed.

As I had hoped, the police had recovered from the first shock and were trying to head us off. I swung the wheel again and we veered away from the officers who had started to barricade the road we'd entered on. The Land Rover jolted crazily as we hit a ditch, then landed hard and kept rolling. We were shaken but not hurt.

"Hang on, get low!" I yelled, and pulled my head down behind the wheel as we slammed into the wooden fence and hurtled back onto the road, pieces of the wooden railing bouncing on the car and falling off. I stepped hard on the brakes and pulled the wheel to the left with all my strength, and when I looked again, we were roaring down the center of the paved highway, heading north again.

I risked a quick look to the side and started grinning. The jeep had been stopped near the academy entrance. It was surrounded by angry, shouting police officers and the three men in it were standing up and waving their arms.

I sighed with relief and slowed the Land Rover, pulling it back to the proper side of the road.

We drove for a few moments, no one talking.

Finally Leslie said calmly, "I say, Michael. That was glorious. Remind me never to lend you my car, though."

"At least that should keep them busy for a while," I said. "Did they see which way we headed? Does anyone know?"

"I don't think they saw us after we passed them," said Choy-lin. "That was frightening for a moment, wasn't it?"

"We're okay now."

"Where to, old boy?" Leslie asked.

"Back to see Boon Song," I said. "They'll spend days trying to figure out which road we turned off."

"Why not try for Bangkok now," asked Leslie. "Petrol low?"

"Right. We can gas up at Boon Song's. He has a couple of gas engines on the log cutters. Also might confuse our friends back there."

We settled down and drove in silence for a few minutes, me hurrying the Land Rover along.

"I think I must tell you, Michael," Choy-lin said. "I was terribly scared back there."

"Hell," I said. "We all were."

Leigh laughed uproariously, and we came to the shrine and swung off the road and headed for the sawmill.

I lay in the darkness thinking about the last few hours.

Boon Song had met us with open arms, as I knew he would. He was curious about the others, equally curious about the dents in the Land Rover where I had taken it through the fence. But he was far too polite to ask questions.

Instead he fed us and filled us with Thai beer and good conversation. He was still using elephants to get the teak down from the mountains; there didn't seem to be a better

way. Otherwise the mill was running on gasoline and goodwill
and he couldn't have been happier. He promised all the gas
we needed. Later on he showed us his newest son, with his
wife giggling behind her plump hand and her eyes dancing in
pride. Then he took us on a tour of the mill. It was much
larger than I remembered and growing all the time. Before
dusk he led us to the edge of the mill, several hundred yards
from his own home, to a guest house he had built. He had
even piped in water from the river through an intricate
arrangement of bamboo stalks, arranged so the water would
flow by gravity-fall until it reached a tank behind the guest
house. The house was up on stilts, in deference to the
monsoons, and had several bedrooms.

I turned on the bed and stared up into the dark. Outside I
could hear crickets and once, in the distance, an elephant
roaring into the night in love or protest or both, and then it
was quiet again. Across the room Leslie was sleeping quietly
and Choy-lin was in a separate room on the other side of the
guest house. Leigh was in a room near hers. Against my will
I wondered how often they'd shared the same room, the
same bed. That led me to the picture of her as I first saw
her, in a clinging sheath and beautiful enough to take your
breath away. Damn Leigh. And what was his game, anyway?

Why not find out right now?

I swung my legs over the side of the bed and stood up and
drew on my pants. As I was slipping on my shoes there was a
scratching at the open doorway and as I looked at it I saw
the curtains covering the doorway part and Leigh's tall figure
stood there. Beyond him I could see the night, bright with
moonlight. He had come in from outside and was trying to
adjust to the darkness of the room. I stood very still and in a
few minutes he saw me, a little startled to see me standing
up. With a movement of his head he gestured me outside.

I moved through the curtains and followed him out onto
the small porch and down the wooden steps to the ground
below. At the bottom of the steps we stopped and looked at
each other. He put one finger over his lips to warn me to be
silent, then wheeled and walked away from the guest house,
keeping in the shadows of the trees and moving in the
direction of the river. When I was sure we weren't seen, I
walked after him, hurrying to keep up with his long-legged
stride.

He slipped into the undergrowth and disappeared in the

dark. I went in where he did, hoping the cobras were sacked out for the night, and came out the other side to see him standing on a little knoll, hands in pockets, and staring out across the river. The river looked clean and cold in the moonlight and there was a slight breeze, which kept the mosquitoes away. I watched him standing there, for a moment, trying to sort out my feelings. He turned and spoke, the first time I had ever heard his voice without urgency in it, or the feigned insanity.

For I was sure the insanity was a pretense.

"Michael Hawkins," he said softly. "It's been quite a long time since we've really talked with each other, hasn't it?"

I walked up to him and he held out his hand and I took it. We shook hands solemnly and he said, "I want to thank you, Michael, for all you've done and apologize for all the trouble I've caused."

"It's all right," I said. "Everyone seems to think it's worth it."

"Let's sit down," he said. We sat a little apart on the knoll and looked into the river for a few seconds.

"I was just on my way to see you," I told him. "I was going to admit to a great deal of confusion. Something I wouldn't do if I were sure you were insane."

The moonlight was bright enough for me to see his smile.

"I am no more insane than any man," he said softly, "if you speak in general terms. You might say that politically I spent a dozen crazy years in China. You might also say that I have no regrets for most of them, but despite that, I will admit to having made a mistake. There was an obsession that perhaps was a form of insanity."

"What was that?"

"Believing in man's innate goodness, in the beginning. And after that thinking one man could change the world." He paused. "And after that, Michael, realizing that all ideologies, whatever their lofty beginnings, are focused on one end—the perpetuation of that ideology, no matter what the cost."

"If you believe that why are you swapping sides? What difference would it make?"

He took his time answering.

"Because of the information I have," he said. "I can only hope that the West won't reach the point that it sets the world on fire. I know what China intends to do."

I wet my lips. "This is why you left?"

"Yes. China must be stopped. I can help."

"Frankly, Leigh," I said, "you seem to have taken your time about deciding which side you're on."

"There were complications. Oh, I don't blame you for being a bit put off. After all, I've been in the enemy camp for quite a while. All I can tell you is that everything in my life led me to that position. And only intellect—remember that, Michael—only intellect could lead me away. Emotionally, a great part of me is still in China, will always be in China."

"Why the phony madness?" I asked. "I can't understand that."

"Let me start at the beginning."

"Okay," I said. "We've got all night, and I'm curious."

Leigh lay back in the grass and stared up at the sky. I sat on the knoll, watching him and waiting. He put his hands behind his head and his eyes looked off into the distance, looking over the years.

"It began in England, with a toy horse. I had one and a playmate didn't. His family couldn't afford toys for him and I could not understand why. I had everything I wanted. I was only a child, of course, but I never forgot it, because it seemed to happen again and again as I grew older. A friend wasn't able to go to camp with me. Another friend couldn't afford a car, or to take girls the places I could take them. My parents believed they were being very democratic, of course, letting me associate with the less fortunate. All they were doing was giving me a social conscience.

"It went on and on and became more and more frustrating. I was heading for a job in the Foreign Office and my dear mother was picking out a bride. One day I looked at my classmates. Like me, they were all well-educated snobs, all in a pattern that would lead them into the Establishment and places of prominence and they tried not to think at all about the working classes. I became sick of it and looked around for something useful to do. I thought if I got a job, perhaps, it would make me feel a bit more necessary. I went to Fleet Street and became a journalist and eventully was classed as a radical. I got involved in a few rebellious causes and got the sack from the paper. Then, one night in Soho, I met a man in a pub who said he'd been watching me and would I like to work for the *Daily Worker*?

"I won't bore you with the next few years; they were rather much alike except for one thing: unlike most people, I didn't merely embrace communism. I fell in love with it. The great, glowing promise of it that would allow everyone to have all they needed, all the food and the freedom from hunger, and the decency of deciding one's own life work, and all that. Even a toy horse for each child. God, it promised so much!"

I looked away. There was pain in his eyes and voice. I kept my eyes on the river while he continued.

"From a mild sort of radical I became an impatient revolutionist. I made a trip to Russia and came back enthralled with the possibilities. Even then, you will notice, I was enchanted with possibilities, not with what was happening in Russia at that very moment. You might say I lost my journalistic objectivity.

"Then the war erupted in Korea. I volunteered as a journalist, but the *Daily Worker* had no money. I paid my own way to Asia. I had some money left over from an inheritance. I used capitalistic money to get me to Asia to work for communism, but the irony of it escaped me at the time. You may remember me at Panmunjom—appeared rather cool, I believe, but my mind was in a ferment. Here was a confrontation I could understand, or thought I could. It came down to conflicting ideologies in which men, in the end, picked up weapons and went out to die for their beliefs. Or so it seemed at the time. I don't know. I only know that I signed on with Hsinhua as a correspondent and covered the war. I remembered you from Panmunjom, remembered you very well. You seemed a decent enough sort. I remember thinking at the time that I could trust your information, could trust you. Later on I came to the point where there was no one around me I could believe in, and I thought of you often. When the time came to leave, I thought if I could just see you again, just get some assurance from you that all would be well, then I could leave China. On top of that the information I had made it imperative I get out. But I suppose I was just human enough to want decent treatment. At any rate, I thought of you. And here we are."

"Here we are," I repeated. "But that doesn't cover everything."

"No. There are a few details left out."

"Like the information you have."

"I thought perhaps Mr. Trent might have told you about that."

"No, he's careful. As a matter of fact, maybe I shouldn't know. I guess what I really want is for you to tell me all this is worth the effort."

In the darkness I could see his tired smile.

"Believe me, Michael"—his voice was almost a whisper—"it's worth it."

I didn't know what to say to him.

After a while he started talking again. "I wish I could tell you," he said, "about the mystique and the miasma of China. I wish I could tell you about the way the skies are, and the earth, and how in China the whole sum of man's struggle can be seen in one man's attempt to scratch a subsistence from the soil. There is space, in China, and time. There are Chinese mountains—you'd have to see them—mountains that look like the drawings of a child, coming up on the horizon after you've trekked across a desert. Mountains with snow on them.

"I wish I could tell you about the changing face of it. I'm not sure that even the Chinese understand the Chinese. Even now, talking with you here, Michael, trying to get away from China, I can get excited about the emergence of new ideas, new experiments in living with one another. Ah, well. Doesn't do much good to talk about it now, does it?"

I didn't try to answer. I just sat there, listening.

"If you are a man," he began again, "who loves, who loves humanity but can't stand it one at a time—are you like that, Michael?"

"No," I said. "I like a lot of people, one at a time. The concept of humanity goes beyond me, I'm afraid."

"Well, it's like this. If you are a man who loves humanity, you are prepared to excuse all sorts of excesses, committed in the name of humanity. You are prepared, in the end, to condone murder in the name of love, to support wars in the name of religion.

"I did that.

"Trent has probably told you about me. I went to Hsinhua and drifted into Intelligence. I arrived at that point where I knew—I knew, Michael—as much as any man about China's aspirations. I can't deny that I supported them. For humanity, of course."

He paused and I asked, "What happened?"

"I'm not the first to become disenchanted with communism," he said slowly. "But I thought I was different. Strange

—I wasn't different at all. When I realized how monstrous it had become, I realized also that I had to leave it. God, you must think me naive!"

"For a man of your intellect I don't think you were very bright," I said.

"True. But you see, I believed man was basically something fine and decent."

"And you don't now?"

"Oh, I suppose I do, even now. But I believe his stupidity and greed is a counterbalance so strong that he may never bring about an end to wars and conquest."

"Pretty gloomy, isn't it?"

"Perhaps."

I thought of his letter about China and dragons and mumbled a few lines of it. Leigh looked up in surprise, then nodded.

"You know, Michael, weapons predated man. They're finding that out in Africa now. They're finding out that the use of weapons by killer apes helped jerk man into a crude form of civilization, helped him survive. Man's use of weapons is a legitimate heritage. But there's one big difference now."

"What's that?"

"It isn't a matter of survival anymore. It's a matter of surviving on your own terms. A matter of using weapons to force your particular form of survival on someone else. And you do this only when you are convinced it must be done or you—you, personally—have no reason for survival, for continuing. This, Michael, is what makes China so dangerous. China has arrived at a pivotal moment: it will force its own brand of survival on the world or sacrifice itself. The people who lead China today have no intentions of becoming sacrifices."

Leigh sat up and ran his hand through his hair. He looked tired and for the first time I realized what a strain this had been on him.

"It won't be long now, Leigh," I said. "We'll have you and Choy-lin out and away and you can start a normal sort of life." I hoped I sounded comforting.

Leigh looked at me for a long moment. "Now we're reaching a rather crucial point," he said. "I want to get away from it, to live normally again. I can't do it in England, I'm afraid. Can I do it in America?"

"I'm sure you can," I said confidently.

"Can Choy-lin?"

"Why not?" I said. "I don't see any problem."

"Well, as a matter of fact, there is."

"Okay, tell me. We'll hash it out."

"It goes back to your earlier question. Why did I pretend to be insane? Wasn't that what you asked?"

"Yes, and I'm glad you brought it up again. I'm curious as hell."

"What do you know of Choy-lin?"

The question caught me by surprise.

"Not a hell of a lot," I said. "Her parents were killed by the Communists. She's apparently adept at learning languages. She's in love with you, I guess. She's coming over with you. That's about it."

Leigh nodded. "I knew very little about her in the beginning," he said. "She came to me, needing love. Because we both spoke English and because she held a minor clerical job in a building where Hsinhua had a branch office. She showed me pictures of her parents, killed by the Communists, she said. She was taking a rather tremendous risk in confiding to a Hsinhua official."

I thought of her, taking such a risk. I could believe it.

"She became a companion, then a mistress, if they still use that word these days. We were very close. We had several years of great fun and warmth and love before I decided to . . . to defect."

He stopped again and the silence grew. I could sense he was looking for exactly the right words.

"I caught her by surprise with the decision to leave China. She wasn't expecting it. By the time we got to Canton, she had accepted it, or so I thought. Then your man in Canton was killed and I had a terrible several hours when I realized why and how. I had led them to him—because I myself had been betrayed."

The warning buzzer suddenly kicked off, loud and insistent.

"It kept happening. When we couldn't get out of Canton to run for the border at Hong Kong, I had to find a way to confuse them, to delay, to make unexpected moves. I couldn't become ill—that would mean no traveling. I couldn't leave her. Frankly, I couldn't leave her because I love her. Does that surprise you?"

"No," I said.

"It seemed that everywhere we went, Hsinhua or some other apparat was looking for us. I began to feign moments of irrationality because I didn't want Choy-lin to know that I suspected her.

"What I hoped for—what I still hope for—is to take her out with me. I'm sure she can adjust to life in the United States. I think I can make her happy."

I had a terribly empty feeling in my stomach.

"Are you trying to say, Leigh, that Choy-lin is a spy? An enemy agent?"

He looked me full in the face. "Yes," he said, "I'm sure now that she's been spying on me for years. But I think I can win her over, if"—he stood up, suddenly excited—"if you help me. We mustn't tell Trent. He won't believe she can change."

I got to my feet. "If I read you right," I said, "you pretended to be insane just to keep moving, to keep Choy-lin with you without her knowing you suspected her, to fake Leslie out of the picture until you could get Choy-lin to the States? Is that right? Is that it, Leigh?"

My voice had risen and my fists were clenched. He was shaken and he took a step back before he answered, "Yes."

"Do you realize," I nearly shouted, "how many men have died to get you out of China? It's too damned late to change that, but from here on out she's going south under guard. And you're going on whether you like it or not."

We stood facing each other on the edge of the river. I was conscious of the night sounds and the quickening breeze.

"Michael——" he began, but never finished the sentence.

There was gunshot booming in the night and the sound of an engine starting, and gears raking as a vehicle shot out of the edge of the camp.

I sprinted for the underbrush, Leigh right behind me.

On the other side of the brush Leslie stood with a gun in his hand.

"What the hell?" I said.

"Choy-lin," he said. "She's stolen the Land Rover."

"Oh, God, oh, God," Leigh breathed, the pain audible in his voice.

"What happened, Leslie?"

"I saw you leave with Leigh and decided to tag along. But I wasn't fast enough. Choy-lin was in front of me, keeping in the shadows. I moved away from her and we hit the bushes here about the same time. When it started to become clear that she's a Red Chinese Intelligence agent, I worked my way through the bushes toward her, but she'd gotten a head start. The Land Rover pulled out with her in it and it was too damned late. I tried a shot, but the light's too bad."

Around us I could hear the entire community coming awake. A light flickered on in Boon Song's house.

"Where is she going, do you suppose?" Leigh asked.

"My guess is that she's going out to turn up our three ugly friends in the jeep," I replied.

"Michael. Listen to me," Leslie said as he grabbed my sleeve. "Did you refuel the Land Rover when we got here?"

"No. No, I didn't."

"Good show!" he yelled. "She can't get far. She's almost out of petrol! Can we borrow a car here somewhere?"

"Sure," said Boon Song. He had come up in the darkness, unnoticed.

"Boon Song, my friend, my good friend," I said. "It is very important. We must have a vehicle of some sort. Right away."

"Take my jeep, of course," he said. "It does not require a key. It is on the other side of my home. Be careful, Michael. There is something very strange here."

We bolted for the jeep, leaving Boon Song watching worriedly.

I slid behind the wheel and Leigh folded himself into the back. As Leslie swung into the front seat I had the motor turning over. I dropped the clutch and we spun onto the dirt road. When the headlights came on, I headed the jeep straight down the road, hoping there'd be no elephants with wanderlust in the way. I held my eyes on the road and tried not to think about anything but driving. From the corner of my eye I could see Leslie, his face tense, and once I glanced around to see Leigh leaning forward with an expression of almost unbearable pain on his face.

──────────────── eleven

SHE WASN'T ON THE SAWMILL ROAD.
We crossed the bridge and made it to the paved road, but there was no sign of her.

"She's pulled off on one of the logging rails," I said.

"But why, why should she run?" Leigh asked.

"I'll tell you why," I said angrily. "She's trying to get to her friends and bring them back to you, or at least set up a blockade somewhere. She's not nearly as ready to go pro-Western as you might hope, Leigh."

"I can make her see things the way they are," he said stubbornly.

Leslie answered that, his voice surprisingly gentle. "She does that now, I'm afraid. She's the enemy and you know it. In a way she's stronger than all of us. This must have been extremely hard on her, you know, coming into enemy territory this way, running a tremendous risk just to stop you."

I had another thought and it angered me. "She broke that buffalo's leg," I said. "Deliberately."

"She was trying to slow us down, of course," Leslie replied.

"Did you suspect her?"

"No. But I knew someone close to the operation had to be tipping off the other side. Baffling, wasn't it?"

I turned the jeep off onto a logging road. "Might as well start looking for her down one of these roads."

"She'll have stopped somewhere and made off on foot," said Leslie.

"But where?" Leigh asked.

"My guess is back to the police academy to see if her friends are jugged there and what can be done about it. If not there, she'll catch a Thai bus into Korat and look around

144

and then head for Bangkok, for Don Muang, to see if she can stop us."

"Damned clear she isn't on this one," I said, "Shall we keep looking here or take a chance and head for Korat?"

"Let's try a few more trails," Leslie said.

We went down two more, both flat and hard from the elephants' trekking to the river each day, pulling the fantastic loads of teak logs.

"We're in luck," said Leslie as we started down the third. "There it is."

The Land Rover was pulled off to the edge of a trail, almost hidden in the low-hanging brush. I pulled the jeep in front of it, leaving the lights burning but turning the engine off. We scrambled out of the jeep and ran to the Land Rover and I threw open the door on the driver's side. It was empty.

"God damn it," Leslie swore. "She's gotten away on foot."

"You're wrong, Mr. Trent." The voice came from behind us.

We whirled and saw her standing there, just a few feet away. In the light spilling over from the jeep's lights, and in the soft moonglow, we could see the pale loveliness of her face and the taut alertness of her body.

And the long-barreled gun in her hands.

I had no idea how long we stood there, the four of us caught in a suspended moment, a tableau, all actors, playing our roles. I wasn't thinking of anything at all and my nerves seemed to have deserted me. I was strangely relaxed.

I heard Leslie sigh.

"Choy-lin," he said with great calmness. "You can't win. We're going to get Leigh out. No matter what you do. If you put that gun away and help us, I'll do everything I can for you."

"There's nothing you can do for me," she said. "He's not going out. He knows too much. He's been my assignment for years."

Leigh began whispering, over and over, a litany, "Choy-lin, Choy-lin——"

"Shut up, Leigh." Leslie's voice lashed at him.

Leigh was silent again and Leslie turned to me. "Do you recognize that gun?" he asked.

"Yes. It's Boon Song's old elephant gun. She must have taken it from the porch."

"Enough talking," she said. "I——"

Leslie interrupted her. "What kind of gun is it, Michael? I can't see it very well here."

"A double-barreled shotgun. An old one, two triggers and hammers on the outside."

"Enough," she said furiously. "Enough talking. You will listen to me now and do as I say."

Leslie ignored her. He turned to me and I was shocked by the strangeness of his eyes, a look of longing and urgency and pain. His face was set and pale.

"Michael," he said, very low and even. "The time has come. I knew it would someday. I've no regrets. But it's up to you now. It's up to you."

"I don't understand, Leslie," I heard myself whisper. "For God's sake, what are you talking about?"

"Listen to me now, Michael. She's got a problem. There are three of us, but she can only fire twice without reloading." His eyes bored into mine and his voice rose. "Start thinking, Michael."

Then I understood.

"Leslie," I said, "Les."

Choy-lin suddenly stirred.

"Good-bye, chum," Leslie said.

He turned and ran straight for Choy-lin.

A split second later I dived for Leigh.

The first shot caught Leslie full in the chest. It knocked him backward and off his feet and he hit the ground on his back.

The second shot went where Leslie had known it would. She swung the heavy gun in a short arc and fired it point-blank at Leigh.

I hit him first, bowling into him hard to get him out of the way of the blast. It hit me instead.

I felt the heavy pellets tear across my back under the skin, ripping and searing and creating their own shock waves. I went down, bleeding heavily. Leigh crumpled under me, then started dragging himself free. From the corner of my eye I saw Choy-lin throw down the empty shotgun and dart for the jeep. She had failed to stop Leigh; now she was going for help. The jeep would get her as far as she needed to go.

I had strength enough for one shout: "Leslie's gun!"

Leigh stumbled over to where Leslie lay on his back. He

found the pistol right away, in Leslie's jacket pocket. Choy-lin was almost to the jeep.

"Shoot," I said, and as I kept repeating it the word took all my strength and I realized I was whispering: "Shoot, shoot, shoot . . ."

But he didn't.

He stood there with the gun in his hand as she reached the jeep and swung inside. Even then he could have stopped her with one shot. But he didn't fire.

I managed to grasp the fender of the Land Rover and with a great deal of pain pull myself to a sitting position. My whole back was bloody and I felt very faint.

I sat leaning back against the Land Rover, delirious with pain and somehow detached. I watched Leigh lower the pistol and hang his head as the jeep spun away into the night. I tried to speak to him, but I couldn't find my voice.

Finally I rolled down on the ground again, in much pain now, and started dragging myself over to where Leslie lay. He hadn't moved since the shotgun had knocked him there. When Leigh saw me moving, he came over to help.

"Leave me alone," I whispered; I thought it was a shout.

I reached Leslie on my own.

The shot had been at very close range, so all the pellets were grouped and the hole in his chest was wide and ugly. There was no expression at all on his face, but his eyes were open. I couldn't bear to look at them after the first glance. His blood was all over the ground and now, too, was a great deal of mine.

I rolled over on my back, not caring anymore. At that precise moment I truly didn't give a damn if I lived or died. It was all the same to me.

Leigh bent over me. "You've got to see a doctor," he said.

I stared at him and searched for whatever strength I could find. "Why didn't you shoot?" I asked quite clearly.

He looked away. "I couldn't," he said. "I couldn't do it."

I felt my body getting lighter, felt the darkness around me. "You son of a bitch," I said, and passed out.

When I opened my eyes again, I saw the ceiling of Boon Song's clinic. My throat was dry, but otherwise I felt fine. Until I moved. I tried to sit up and the pain went lancing across my shoulders. Only then did I feel the tightly wrapped bandages around my chest. I lay back down and moved my arms and legs. They were all right. I seemed to be all right except for the soreness across the back of my shoulders where the pellets had gone.

I wet my lips and croaked, "Leigh?"

In a moment I heard footsteps outside and Boon Song came in, looking at me worriedly. "I am pleased that you are awake, Michael. Mr. Leigh also is quite worried about you. You lost much blood, the doctor says."

"Where's Leigh?"

"In the guest house. He is sleeping. He is very tired from carrying you back here."

I thought about that.

"What about Leslie, Boon Song?"

"We buried him on a hill by the river, Michael. We gave him a proper funeral, but nobody had a Bible, so we could not read over him, so I said a few things about what a nice man he was. Do you think that was all right?"

I looked away so he wouldn't see my face. After a while I could answer him without my voice breaking. "He would have wanted that very much, Boon Song. I'm sure he would have preferred that."

Boon Song brightened. "It is a nice spot. From it you can see the river in both directions. Sometimes our young women go to that very spot to bathe. Do you think he would have liked that?"

"I'm sure of it," I smiled. "He was very fond of women."

"But it was a woman that killed him, was it not? I am very confused about the people you brought here, Michael. Mr. Leigh will not talk about it."

"I'll tell you all about it someday. How long have I been here?"

Boon Song glanced at his watch. "About five or six hours."

I struggled and sat up. "I need all your help now," I told him. "Not only to get us out of here but to protect you and your family. Some very nasty men will be coming here to look for Mr. Leigh and me. If we are gone, you won't be bothered. If we're still here, I'm afraid someone innocent could be hurt. You perhaps. Or one of the kids."

"I am not afraid, but I will help you, in any case. What do you require?"

"A jeep again. Any map you may have of the back roads. Plenty of gas."

"I will see to it. When would you like to leave?"

"Now," I said, and clenched my teeth and got out of bed and started dressing. It took a while.

When I stepped out of the clinic, the jeep was waiting. Leigh sat behind the wheel, looking old and tired. He nodded to me but didn't speak.

"Hang on," I said. "I'll be back in a minute."

Boon Song knew instinctively what I wanted. He gestured up the hill to the right and I started climbing, panting and feeling the tight bandages and hoping I wouldn't start the blood flowing again.

The grave was under a tree near the top of the hill, looking down on the river. Someone had fashioned a crude wooden cross at the head of it. I sat down beside it and listened. The wind was singing across the mountains and I could hear the ripple of water over the rocks and downstream the laughter of small boys splashing in the water. Upstream an elephant was washing himself, blowing water and pausing occasionally to swing his ponderous head from side to side. I sat there and listened to the noises and felt the wind bending the long grass and the sun hot on my face despite the wind.

Men in Leslie's profession didn't get medals. They just lived for what they believed in, and when the time came, they died for it.

It's up to you, he had said, it's up to you.

I went back down the hill and shook hands with Boon Song and got into the jeep. I turned to Leigh. "Head out to the road," I ordered. "I'm taking you out."

Without a word he started the engine and the jeep rolled out of the sawmill settlement and out toward the road that leads south.

———————— twelve

WE DIDN'T SPEAK UNTIL WE REACHED THE
paved road and Leigh asked, "Now what?"

"See anything?" I grunted.

"No."

"Then, take the paved road till I tell you where to turn."

He did and we rode on, alert and watchful.

I sat slightly forward; it hurt like hell when I leaned back.
Leigh missed as many of the holes in the road as possible,
but I think I felt every turn of the wheels.

A few miles from the sawmill road intersection I pointed
to another side road and Leigh pulled off onto it. We bumped
along, with me swearing and Leigh busy with the gearshift
and the wheel. It lasted for a good two hours before I felt
safe enough to get back on the paved road again, but when
we did, we had gotten around Korat and any traps that
might have been set in the city.

"What's next?" Leigh asked.

"A good question. We're a hundred and twenty kilometers from Bangkok. Don Muang is on the outskirts. Let's
figure on being there just about dusk. Unless, of course, we
run into trouble along the way." I paused. "I sort of hope we
do, too, Leigh. You know?"

He nodded. "I can't tell you how guilty I feel. I won't even
attempt to say the right thing. I just want you to know that
I'll do whatever has to be done from here on out. Whatever
it is."

After a while I said, "All right. One thing I want right now
is an indication that you're worth Leslie's death. He's told me
how bright you are and what a marvelous intellect and all
that." I turned to him and said savagely, "Prove it to me.
Now."

"You hate me, don't you?"

"Oh, hell, I don't suppose so," I said, leaning back wearily

150

in spite of the pain. "A lot of people got killed for you, and it's not over yet. We're heading right into it again. I just get the feeling you'd have to know everything about Red China to make it all worthwhile."

We rolled another quarter of a mile before he answered.

"All right, Michael. In my own defense, I'll give you a sample."

"Good. But keep an eye out while you're talking."

"Right."

Then he asked, "What do you know of China's nuclear potential?"

"Damned little," I confessed.

"You and everyone else. Shall we discuss that?"

"Why not?"

"Lop Nor is in Sinkiang, the end of the world. China has fired off three nuclear explosions there. In October of 1964, May of 1965 and May of 1966. The last one was two hundred kiloton, ten times more powerful than the first two but still not big enough to worry about. But it had an interesting aspect in that it indicated a capability of producing a hydrogen weapon that the West refers to as the three-stage bomb, the fission-fusion-fission bomb.

"It's detonated by a fission trigger that causes a thermonuclear fusion reaction, and that fissions a natural uranium bomb jacket. There is absolutely no limit to its power. At this moment there are at least two thousand scientists working on various facets of producing this weapon in China right now. There's a diffusion plant at Lanchow capable of producing fissionable material.

"America isn't worried about Red China's nuclear power right now, under the impression that there are no adequate means of delivering the bomb anywhere. I remember reading one of your intelligence reports; the gist of it was that if China delivered a bomb, it would be either by IL-28 light jet bombers, which are limited to something like seven hundred miles, or by the Soviet-type TU-4, which can take it out two thousand miles. That wouldn't get it to America, you know."

"Go on," I said.

"Your Secretary of Defense believes China can launch an attack on countries with a five hundred-mile range in two or three years. Your C.I.A. believes it would take another decade before China could launch a nuclear warhead against the United States by way of rockets or missiles." Leigh turned to look at my face. "They're wrong, Michael.

"China can do it now. I know how and from where and what the timetable would be. I also know, as much as any man in China, what it would take to restrain China from using the bomb—or push her into it."

"Well," I said finally, "You've convinced me."

"Rather easy," he smiled. "You didn't even let me get to the part involving the Party battle to pick Mao's successor, or the new plan to start all over again in Indonesia, or the two states where China plans to launch new and simultaneous 'wars of national liberation.' "

"Christ," I said, "No wonder Choy-lin tried to shoot you."

"Yes. That had me puzzled for a bit. Then I realized that in the period she thought I was mad, she had hopes for getting me back and salvaging me. When she found out I was sane, she had to stop me."

"And when Leslie forced the issue, she realized, with only two chances, that one of them should be to eliminate you."

"I won't forget you saved my life."

"What I don't want you to forget, Leigh, is that Leslie gave up his. For you."

"I know that," he said thoughtfully.

"Let me drive for a while."

We had been very lucky. In the long afternoon we were one of the very few vehicles on the road. The others had been the distinctive Thai buses, unbelievably packed with passengers and obviously no threat. I began to get the feeling that they had decided it was too risky trying to find us on the road now, especially since the monsoon's edge was still north of where we were now and we could make good time. Instead they would be waiting at Don Muang.

They would be watching the embassy car and the waiting airplane. The most dangerous time for us would be the moment we leaped from the jeep and got into the embassy car. They would try to stop us then, when we were without protection. It would have to be very fast. Once we got into the plane, we were safe. But it would be very tricky because I had only a vague idea where the car would be. Perhaps a better plan would be to roll the jeep right across the apron and out to the plane without bothering with the embassy staff car. I moved my arms and felt the pull in my shoulders and back; I wasn't going to be able to move very fast anyway.

We didn't talk much after that; we just pushed the jeep hard and pointed it south and kept going. I couldn't remember what day it was. I had the feeling we'd been going south half of my life.

Jerry Ward, dead in Cu Chi, Vietnam, from fragments of an exploding mine while covering the war. Leslie Trent, dead in northeast Thailand, of a shotgun blast in the chest at close range, while attempting to smuggle an extremely important personage to freedom. At least Leslie died instantly. In this case I knew it wasn't a lie.

"Your turn to drive," I said.

We passed Sara Buri, with me convinced now they would be waiting at the airport. There were more klongs now with people on them, and more water in the klongs. There had been some rain this far south, but the monsoon was still in the northeast and several days away from Bangkok. Along the roads now were small settlements and clusters of stores and shops. I knew that from here on in there would be more and more people and buildings. If we were going to come up with any sort of strategy, it would have to be soon.

I lit a cigarette and tried to think.

"It's getting on toward dusk," Leigh said.

"Yeah. Look, let's pull off and sit and think for a minute."

He nodded and turned the wheel, then jerked it back suddenly at a shout beside us. We had almost hit a sam lor driver, pedaling a fat customer along the road. I shrugged my apologies and the driver kept pedaling away, glancing back at us and muttering. Leigh stopped the jeep and we sat there staring through the windshield at the disappearing sam lor.

"Michael," Leigh asked suddenly, "would you listen to a wild idea?"

It took us an hour. By then it was dark.

Leigh sat on the seat of the sam lor, testing the pedals. He had rolled up his pants and taken off his socks. The dirty, sweat-stained shirt was authentically Thai, and so was the conical hat worn low over his eyes. Except for his size, he'd fit in, at night, with the thousands of other sam lor drivers in and around Bangkok.

I had changed shirts also. Blood had soaked through the bandages and on into the shirt I had worn south, so a new one had been necessary. I couldn't find any logical headgear except a beret. Sitting in the back of the sam lor, I looked like a very, very minor functionary, too lazy to walk.

Leigh would pedal and I would ride. I made that decision because I couldn't pedal very far with the back wounds, and also because if we didn't make it, they would have a tendency to shoot into the sam lor and ignore the driver—at least I thought they would.

I wasn't trying to be a hero, either. I kept remembering Leslie and damned well meant to get Leigh on that airplane.

The sam lor and the clothing came from a delighted shop owner on the road between Sara Buri and Don Muang. He was so anxious to take the jeep in an even swap that he didn't even bother to bargain and his greed got the better of his Thai good manners. I didn't want to think about the vehicles I owed people in this country by now.

I gave Leigh directions to Don Muang and had him repeat them. We couldn't be calling back and forth every time a turn had to be made, so we worked out a system. He knew the general direction. If he started to make a wrong turn, I cleared my throat. If I didn't, he kept pedaling. I hoped his legs would hold out. So did he.

Fortunately we insisted on a sam lor with a light. It was quite dark when we headed for the airport and there was plenty of traffic on the road. I sat back and for a moment managed to enjoy the Thailand night, with its mysterious tinkling noises and lights and soft, musical voices. But I soon gave that up and started thinking about the airport again. We'd have to take our chances now. There was nothing more we could do.

Leigh glanced back at me once. His face was flushed, and sweat completed the darkening of his shirt, but he kept pedaling. I had a momentary sense of irony—one of the world's most sought after men was breathing hard and pedaling a sam lor through the darkness, with me for a passenger.

I grunted a couple of times when Leigh started in the wrong direction. He corrected our course and kept going.

When I saw the airport lights, I began to get tense. Whatever would happen to us now would happen in the vicinity of those lights and in the next few minutes. I got out the Luger and slipped a round up into the chamber and put it back in my pocket, keeping my hand on it.

Leigh stopped the sam lor and walked back, pretending to

examine a wheel. "We're almost there," he whispered. "Any ideas?"

"Just what I told you," I answered softly. "Pedal right out to the plane. Ignore the car. Maybe we can fake them out."

"And if we don't?"

"Get off and go like hell for the plane and don't look back. If you get inside, slam the hatch and tell them to take it up."

He glanced into the cab where I was sitting, but he couldn't see my face. I saw his lips tighten, his eyes narrow.

"Don't argue, Leigh. If you don't get on that aircraft, it's all for nothing."

He nodded and got back on the sam lor's bicycle seat and we went around the traffic circle by Don Muang airport entrance, moving easily on the level ground and headed toward the south end of the terminal building.

From the front side of the terminal it is impossible to see the flight line. We had planned just to round the corner—we'd get that far without being suspect, at least—then try for the aircraft, wherever it was spotted.

There were quite a few cars by the terminal.

I didn't see anything that looked suspicious or dangerous.

Then we were around the corner of the terminal and I saw the plane.

It sat at our end of the runway, a sleek and modern aircraft but without a mark on it. Air America again. The hatch in the side facing us was open. I estimated the distance at some 200 yards.

"Leigh," I called, knowing no one could hear us out on the apron. "Go slow for a few minutes, then if we're spotted, go like hell."

He nodded without looking back.

I pulled out the Luger again and sat in the darkness as we moved. My hand on the gun was shaking slightly and my face felt cold despite the warm night. I had lived this moment over and over in my imagination and here it was, finally, and every bit as bad as I thought it would be.

At that moment I saw the car.

It had been parked in the shadows, but now it was moving out very fast and swinging around the fence by the terminal. It was a Renault, one of the Dauphine models, and it was coming very fast now, with its lights off, making for us in a straight line.

"Take off," I yelled. Leigh slammed on the brakes of the

sam lor and leaped off the seat on the other side, away from the car. I heard his shoes sharp on the hard concrete and he ran for the plane.

The car was still out of range, but for comfort I propped my wrist up on the braces supporting the sam lor's cloth roof and squeezed the trigger.

There was a tremendous bang from the Luger and the casing ejected straight up, hit the roof of the sam lor, and fell back on my wrist, burning it slightly. Still, the noise made me feel better and I fired again, watching the Renault bearing down on me and knowing I was unable to run and unable to hide.

I tore my eyes away from the onrushing car to check Leigh's progress. He was about halfway to the plane and they hadn't seen him yet. They were still heading for me.

But so was another car.

I saw it coming from the other end of the terminal. Like the Renault it was coming on fast and its lights were out. It was a long, low American auto and it started eating up the distance between itself and the Renault.

I watched, fascinated, while the larger car bore down on the smaller one and the smaller one streaked straight at the small and rickety sam lor. Then I recovered and squeezed off a third round.

At that point I found out they were no longer very interested in taking Leigh back alive. They had no idea we weren't both in the back of the sam lor and they were shooting like it didn't make any difference who they hit first.

I dropped down to the floor, a reflexive action that started the blood pouring from my back again. Bullets ripped through the cloth top and shattered the small glass window in the back, sending a shower of glass down on top of me.

I stuck the Luger out the side, staying flat on the floor, and fired again, twice. It didn't even slow them up. The car just kept racing for the sam lor and I suddenly got the notion they were going to ram it.

If I raised my head they'd shoot. If I stayed I'd be rammed.

I decided to stay.

I put my head down on the floor, braced my feet against the wooden planking of the seat, and waited.

There was a terrible crash. I heard it, but I didn't feel a thing. There was the clanging of metal coming together at high speed and falling glass and the rim of a headlight coming loose and rolling away in a wide, slow circle. When I raised my head I saw the small car pushed yards away, crunched in the maw of the heavier sedan. There was blood on the windshield of the American car, but the two men in it appeared to be all right. They were getting out, one of them dazed, and starting for the Renault. I pulled myself up and stepped down from the sam lor. There were three men in the Renault; two of them were mangled but the third was still alive and not badly hurt. He was in shock and had lost his gun somewhere.

I wheeled to see if Leigh had made it to the plane.

Choy-lin was there.

She had been thrown from the wreckage but had recovered quickly. I just had time to notice that her blouse was torn and her lovely shoulder had a long jagged gash in it. She was leaning against the sam lor, steadying herself as she held a pistol in both hands and sighted in on Leigh's back. It was a long shot, but she might have made it. I would never know if she could have hit him or not.

I couldn't take the chance.

I threw up the Luger and fired. She wasn't more than thirty feet away. The slug struck her high and to the right in her back, knocking her completely around. She started down, holding onto the sam lor with both hands, the pistol clattering on the concrete.

I walked over to her. She was on her knees, still holding onto the sam lor. She looked up at me and I saw a quizzical frown, a delicate bending of one lovely eyebrow. As I started to reach down to her she let go of the sam lor and pitched forward on the concrete. Her breathing stopped.

Sirens sounded and the two men from the embassy car loped over, one of them bleeding from a cut on the head.

"Better take off," the other one said. "Thai police all over the place any minute now. Take off; we'll straighten up the mess here."

I turned and started jogging for the Air America plane, feeling the pull in my back with every step. Halfway to the plane two figures dropped from the hatch and ran up to help. Between them they managed to hurry me up to the hatch.

Hands reached down and pulled me on board. Someone inside helped me gently forward in the plane to a seat. The plane already was rolling and someone was fastening a seat belt around me. Whoever did it also reached down and gently pushed the safety on the Luger, still in my hand. I opened my hand and he took the gun away and I put my head back. I was shaking all over.

I felt the plane lift off and opened my eyes. Leigh was sitting across from me, his face pale and his eyes wet with tears. He caught my stare and tried to smile. I'm sure we were thinking the same thing. We were remembering how we'd met in the middle of a war on opposite sides, so many years before. Who knows, I thought, it could have been the other way around.

The plane reached for altitude.

I retched unexpectedly, and someone came with a towel. I tried to apologize but couldn't find the words. I heard someone say "shock" and knew they were talking about me.

I turned my head and opened my eyes again. There was a round window right by my head and I stared out into the night. Below were the lights of a great city, a great Asian city, with color and brilliance in the heart of it and strings of lights running away for miles in all directions. From the plane you couldn't see the klongs and the press of humanity, nor the killers in the jungles, nor the despair in the eyes of the children, nor the farmers grubbing for food in the earth. But then you couldn't see the leprosy clinic, either, and the love behind it. You couldn't see Lynn and her quiet smile and the hope she gave me. You couldn't see the small shrines built in love and reverence, or Boon Song's settlement in the Thai hills. You couldn't see Leslie's grave from the plane. All you could see was the darkness that was the sea and the hills of Asia, and the glow of a vibrant city, slipping toward the horizon.

I closed my eyes and tried to sleep.

5
BIG NEW BESTSELLERS
FROM FAWCETT GOLD MEDAL

Suspense

OPERATION DRUMFIRE
by Dan J. Marlowe   T2541   75¢

Organic Gardening

GARDENING WITH NATURE
by Leonard Wickenden   M2542   95¢
NEWLY REVISED

Sports

OFFICIAL BASEBALL
   RECORD BOOK   P2543 $1.25

Suspense

DIAL M—FOR MONEY
by Donald Taggart   T2544   75¢

Science Fiction

A FOR ANYTHING
   (former title: The People Maker)
by Damon Knight   T2545   75¢